Official

Charmanie Saquea

Chapter 1

Micah

I usually don't say nothing. I sit back and observe, I'm usually the one to think before I react. I guess you can say I'm more level headed than Mykell and Ramone but right now I'm feeling like fuck all that! They took my baby girl away from me. I loved that girl like she was really my flesh and blood, hell you couldn't tell me that she wasn't my blood sister.

I've never been the type of nigga to cry but right now I'm holding back the tears that are threatening to fall. Baby girl didn't deserve to go out like that. Sitting here looking at my little brother ain't making me feel no better. He really loved Neicey, no doubting that. Yea, they had their little issues but I know for a fact that they loved each other unconditionally. I honestly think they could've worked that shit out but Neicey was just too damn stubborn.

Damn, Imma really miss her crazy ass.

"Man, this shit can't be real. She can't be gone," Mykell said bringing me from my thoughts.

"I'm with you baby bruh, this shit don't feel real," I agreed.

"I loved that girl man. It feels like a piece of my heart been ripped out my chest," he stated calmly. Then the next thing I know, he started flipping, throwing things around the room. He ripped his IV out of his arm, and blood started gushing out. The doctors ran into the room to see what all the commotion was about.

"Mr. Jones, were going to need you to calm down," one of the doctors said.

"Fuck that! I just lost my girl and you want me to calm down? Fuck that and fuck you!" he yelled.

Honestly, I've never seen my brother flip out like that. Not even when our mama died, but I guess he was too young to understand then.

Pops just got up and walked over to Kell and held his head in his arms while he cried. He was really bawling crying. The nurse took that as an opportunity to put his IV back in.

Big Ramone's phone started ringing. He looked at it funny before he answered.

"Hello? Yes, this is he."

The room was silent except for Mykell's crying.

"Actually I'm still up here, I'm in my son-in-law's room. Mykell Jones. Alright, that's fine."

"That was weird. That was the doctor that worked on Reneice. He said he has something real important he needs to speak with me about."

"What could it be?" my pops asked. "Do they want you to identify the body again?"

"Good question. I just want him to hurry up so I can go home and get some rest before I start making funeral arrangements. It looks like our grandsons are a little tired too," he said, referring to MJ and baby Romell knocked out sleep. I'm surprised they're still sleep with all the commotion their dad just made.

Five minutes later, a doctor walked into the room. "Hello, my name is Doctor Hall and I worked on Ms. Reneice Peak when she got here. As you know, about an hour ago, I pronounced her dead but it looks like Ms. Peak wasn't ready to go just yet."

I damn near fell out when he said that. *So Neicey's not dead?*

Mykell

I know good and damn well this doctor better not be in here fucking with a nigga's emotions. "So you're telling me that she's not dead? She still alive?" I asked with a little hope in my voice.

"Well yes and no. She did die, but someway her heart started beating again but it was real faint. We waited a little to see if she would stay with us, her heartbeat started to fade again so I took it upon myself to put her on a life support machine until I got the chance to talk to you all," he explained.

"So she alive but the machine is helping her breath?" Micah asked.

"Yes, she also slipped into a coma when her heart started beating again."

"Mack, go get your sister and Ramone. We are going to make this decision as a family," Pops ordered.

"Pops, Big Mone, I think we should keep her on the life support. She came back to us for a reason," I thought.

"I agree," Big Mone said.

Lani and Ramone walked into the room and I could tell both of them had been crying. The doctor told them everything he had explained to us.

"So she's alive?" Ramone asked excitedly.

"Yes but the life support is keeping her alive right now. If you all choose to keep her on the machine it could be pricey. That's why I wanted to see if you wanted to keep her on it."

"YES!" me, Mack and Mone yelled at the same time.

He just smiled, "Alright, then that's settled."

He tried to walk out the room but I stopped him.

"Doc, can I see her please?"

"Are you supposed to be up and moving?" he asked looking concerned.

"No but I really want to see her, just for a minute. Please?" I begged.

"Alright, just for a minute. Then you need to get some rest."

I walked into Neicey's room and was devastated by what I saw. She had tubes running out of her and she looked pale. She looked like she was sleeping peacefully but I just wanted her to wake up so I could see her beautiful smile with those dimples I love so much.

"How long will she be like this, doc?"

"I can't really say, some people stay in a coma for days, weeks, months, maybe even years."

I went over to the bed and leaned down to kiss her. I wanted to cry so bad because she looked dead. I never been the type of nigga to cry but this shit was getting to me.

"I love you Ma." I said before leaving the room.

That muthafucka gon pay for this shit, no doubt about it.

Ramone

I was so shocked but overjoyed at the news the doctor just gave us. I knew my Ladybug was a fighter, she was too stubborn to die. We decided that we would let Mykell go see her first and spend some time with her. That was his moment.

From what I heard, that bitch nigga Kamil got away. I hope he had enough sense to leave the fuckin country because me, my niggas and my brothers gunning for that nigga head. He got my damn sister laying in a damn coma.

I want to hear the whole story from Kell about what happened earlier but I'll wait until tomorrow. Right now everybody just needs some rest. The person I really need to be talking to right now is Le'Lani. She dropped a big bomb on me a little while ago and I wanted to see what was up with her.

"Alright y'all, I'll be back up here tomorrow to check on Kell and Ladybug. If anything changes or happens, call me immediately."

"We will son. You just go home and get some rest. Today has been a very long and eventful day," Pops said.

"You want me to take MJ or Romell home with us?"

"We'll be fine, you father is taking Baby Mell and I got MJ."

"Cool, well we out," I said taking Lani's hand.

I wasted no time shooting off questions as soon as we got in the car.

"How long have you known? How far along are you? When is your next doctor's appointment? Don't you have to take those pills Ladybug took when she was pregnant?"

"Slow down baby," she laughed for the first time that night. "I haven't even been to the doctor's yet. I took a pregnancy test at home and it came back positive."

"When you wake up tomorrow, yo ass better call the doctor's to make sure everything is okay and see how far along we are."

"We?"

"Yes, we. The last time I checked we made that baby *together* so therefore we're in this together," I said shocking her and myself.

"Awww baby, you're so sweet." She blushed.

"So I've been told," I joked.

*   *   *

The next morning Lani and I went up to the hospital bright and early.

"Who you wanna see first?" I asked as we pulled up to the hospital.

"Neicey," she answered.

"Let's go then."

We made our way to the third floor to see my Ladybug. *This shit is too much like déjà vu, every time I come to this hospital, it's for my sister.*

Lani opened up the curtains to let some sunlight in the room while I went to sit by my sister's side to talk to her. I've been told that they can hear everything you say, they just can't respond.

"Hey Ladybug, that was some scary shit you pulled. I thought I had really lost you. You just don't know how crazy a nigga was going when the doctor told us you were gone. I know we've had some good times and some bad also, but through it all we remained close.

"I've never told you, but I was scared as hell when I took you in after Mama passed. I was just growing up myself and I didn't want to teach you the wrong things or be a bad influence on you. But you turned out real good, better than I expected. I don't regret doing it either, raising you was probably one of the best and most positive things I've ever done in my life. I probably don't tell you enough, but I really am proud of you and the woman you've become Ladybug, I really am. Well that's enough jibber jabber from me."

I got up so Lani could be closer to her.

"Baby, you just go up and see Kell. I think Imma stay down here for a while. I'll meet you up there.

"Aight, that's cool."

I walked out that room feeling like shit, honestly. It's my job to protect my sister and look at what I let happen to her. It's killing me to see my sister like that.

Lani

Just looking at my sister laying in this bed hooked up to a machine is killing me but I have no worries. I know she's going to make it because she's a fighter, her stubborn ass would never leave here and allow Mykell to let another bitch raise her kids. I chuckled at the thought, Reneice would come back and haunt both of their asses.

"Mami, you remember the first day we met? It was like we were meant to be best friends." I laughed at the memory.

I was walking through the mall with texting on my phone when I accidently bumped into somebody. "Damn, bitch! Watch where the fuck you going," I heard a voice say.

I looked up to see three ratchet looking females standing there looking like they didn't even belong in this mall.

"Hold up, you don't know me so watch who you calling a bitch," I said walking up on their asses. Hell, I wasn't scared to fight nobody. I grew up in a house with two older brothers who taught me very well how to defend myself.

"Bitch you will get you ass beat." Never being one to do too much talking, I threw the first punch. We went at it then all of a sudden one of her friends decided to get bold and jump in. I didn't care though, it wasn't the first time I was jumped and probably wouldn't be the last. I never realized that someone was helping me until the mall security and Micah came and broke it up. I

caught the end of the other girl putting a beat down on the ratchet pack's friend. I was pretty impressed.

"She's with me," I said when security grabbed her.

"If you don't leave now, I will call the police," the damn fake ass robo cop said.

"Whatever, c'mon girl," I said picking up my bags and handing them to Micah.

"Yo, what's ya name?" Micah asked.

"Reneice but people call me Neicey," she said.

"Well I'm Mack and this is Lani. You need us to drop you off somewhere or you good?" he asked.

"I'm good but thank you anyways," she said.

"Thanks for looking out back there, that was some real shit you did," I said.

"No problem."

"You're a cutie, we should hang sometime. I really like you."

And that was the start of our sisterhood. "Man Neicey, I will never forget that day. I could just imagine how our two lil asses looked fighting in that damn mall."

I dug in my purse and pulled out a comb and brush and started to comb out her hair. "Neicey, you need to wake up. You know you're about to be a auntie, so you know what that means; nine months' worth of shopping!" I laughed.

"You gon make it through this Reneice. You don't have a choice but to. I will come up here every day and see you until the day you walk up out of here and that's my word."

Chapter 2

Mykell

I wanted to go see Neicey but these nurses acting all stank and shit. Talking about they don't want me to leave the room. If it wasn't for my brother being here, I would've made a run for it.

"Kell just chill. You not gon be in here much longer. Then you'll be able to see her whenever you want to," Micah said trying to be reasonable.

"Aight, man, that nurse just don't want me to go because she want me. She been throwing all types of hints a nigga way." I laughed.

"Nigga, you dumb as hell." Mack laughed with me.

"It's good to see somebody in good spirits," Ramone said walking into the room.

"You know can't nothing keep a boss down," I joked.

"Wassup y'all." He gave both of us a fist pound.

"Why you looking like you just lost yo best friend?" Micah asked.

"Man, Mack. I basically did. I just left Neicey's room and it killed me seeing her like that."

"I know man. I was down there earlier. The doc said if we keep talking to her it could bring her back," Micah agreed.

"Man Kell, what the hell happened in that house?" Mone asked me.

"When I got to the house that nigga was asking her to move to California with him. I straight up told him that wasn't about to happen, then Kya walks her ass in the house from the back door. At this point Neicey going the fuck off, all of a sudden Olivia walks her simple ass in the house talking—"

Micah cut me off. "Whoa, baby bruh! Did you just say Olivia?" he asked shocked.

"Yea man, shit was crazy."

"Who the fuck is Olivia?" Mone asked confused.

"MJ's mom," Mykell responded, unenthused.

"Oh, damn."

"Yea, so like I was saying. She walks in talking about how she baby mama number one and some other bullshit. Come to find out, Kya's dumb ass was working with her the whole time not even knowing Olivia is the bitch I cheated on her with. So she gets to popping off at the mouth, I guess Neicey got tired of her because she pulled her gun out and shot Kya right in the damn head. That's when Olivia asks Kamil why he didn't finish the job and just Kill Neicey. She pulled her gun out and that's when all hell broke loose."

"Well, apparently the police seem to think Neicey took some bullets for yo ass," Micah said.

Ramone's phone rang.

"The third floor, room 328," he said to the caller.

I'm sitting there looking at him like he's crazy, wondering who that was.

"That was Lakey and them. Chill."

"Just wondering," I responded.

"So you're telling me that yo baby mama and yo ex-bitch hired this nigga to kill my sister?" he asked pissed off.

"Pretty much."

"You're also telling me them muthafuckas got away?"

"No worries bruh, they gon get there's"

"Who gon get what?" Lani asked coming into the room holding her stomach.

"What's wrong with you? Why you holding yo stomach?" Mone asked her all concerned and shit.

"Just a little morning sickness." She shrugged.

"WHAT!" Mack and I yelled simultaneously.

"Surprise," she laughed. "You guys are going to be uncles." She beamed.

"You knocked my baby sister up nigga?" I asked Ramone.

"Aye, I didn't say anything when you knocked my baby sister up." He laughed.

"Y'all are so stupid," Lani clowned.

This is the best news I heard all day.

Lakey

Walking into that hospital room and seeing Snook like that had a nigga all fucked up. She didn't even look like herself. I was ready to kill somebody at that moment.

"Damn, this shit ain't supposed to be like this," Corey said

"Hell naw it ain't. This shit gots to be dealt with, no doubt," Howie agreed.

"Oh, it will be. As long as I have breath in my body," I chimed in.

"Let's go see Mone so we can get some more info about this shit," Jason said.

"Yea, let's go."

I couldn't stand looking at her like that. We've known each other all our lives and I've never seen her hurt this bad.

MJ

I can't believe that my mom is laying in a coma. Like I never would have thought I would see the day that she would get hurt something serious like this. My dad and Pop-Pop try to keep me out of the loop but I begged my dad to bring me up here to see my mom. I don't know what my life would be like if she hadn't stepped in when she did. The love she gave me, I didn't receive from my birth mother; wherever she is. Not only did she change my life but my dad's also. She changed him too whether she knows it or not, my dad probably would have ended up back in prison if it wasn't for her; she keeps him well grounded.

I pulled my chair up to her bed to sit down. I grabbed her hand and just sat there listening to the sound of the monitors. Just looking at her like this made me wanna cry. Which is something I've never really did.

"Ma, I need you to wake up. Everybody has been going crazy since you've been like this," I said while rubbing her hand. I sighed before I said something else. "I don't know if I ever told you but…I'm happy you decided to raise me as your son. I know you started off as my auntie Lani's best friend but you became more than that when you and dad got together."

I stopped to wipe away a tear the fell. "I know you two are not on good terms right now but I just want you to know I love you no matter what and you'll always be my mama. I got some basketball games coming up and it won't feel right not having my number one cheerleader there." I chuckled at the thought of her yelling throughout the whole game.

"Fat Fat is getting so big now, he looks just like me and dad but of course I look better." I chuckled. "Alright mom, Imma get up out of here but just know that

I love you and I'll be back." I kissed her forehead before I left the room.

Chapter 3

Lani

I'm now eight months pregnant with a baby girl. I'm on my way to the hospital so I can go see my sister. Nobody has been the same since she's been in that damn coma. My brothers and Ramone are so hell bent on getting revenge, they done hired a damn private investigator to try to help them find Olivia and Kamil.

"Hey, mami. Don't you think it's time for you to wake up now? It's been six months. If you were tired we could've just took us a vacation to get away from them knuckleheads." I chuckled.

I pulled out a brush and comb from my purse and started doing her hair.

"You know your niece will be here next month. Also your brother proposed to me last night girl. It was so cute how he did it. You better be woke by time I pop this little girl out or else I'll never let you live it down. We're supposed to be at home thinking of baby names, doing all that baby shopping and stuff. You know how we do."

I grabbed her hand. "I really love you Neicey. You're more than a friend to me, you're my sister. The only friend I have, you know stuff about me that nobody knows. Please wake up soon, mami. I can't make it without you anymore. Everyone is losing their minds; we're lost without you, especially Mykell and Ramone. MJ misses you and asks about you all the time. He wanted to come see you but he had to go to school.

Romell is so big and handsome now; he looks just like Kell big headed self." I laughed.

"I love you," I said as I kissed her cheek.

When I said that, I felt her squeeze my hand. She's been doing that lately. At first I was scared but the doctor told me that was her was of responding.

"Come back to us soon, mami."

I looked up when I seen Mykell walk in the room.

Mykell

This shit is so stressful. Seeing the one you love laying in a hospital bed and it ain't nothing you can do about it; this shit is killing me slowly. I be wanting to be on some revenge type shit but my pops said that can wait, he said my main priority right now should be helping het Neicey to wake up. He's right. I pulled up to the hospital to go check on Neicey. I really hate coming up here but I know she would do it for me.

"Look, I'm only gon be in here for a second. Stay right here." I said looking over at this chick I been passing time with for a couple of months, her name Candy. She be thinking she wifey or something but I keep reminding her that shit will never be that. I was about to drop her ass off but she got to bitching so I said fuck it.

"Mykell, it's like twenty fucking degrees out here and you want me to sit in the car? Really?"

"Candy please don't get yo ass beat! Now is not the time to be coming all out yo mouth talking shit because right about now I will punch you in the bitch. It's fucking heat in this bitch so what the fuck you complaining for?" I snapped and got out the car without even waiting for an answer.

Sometimes I don't even know why I keep that bitch around. Imma need for Neicey to wake up so we can actually be a family like were supposed to be. This shit is fucking foolishness.

I walked in the room and seen Lani combing Neicey's hair. "Wassup knucklehead?" I said kissing her forehead then kissing Neicey' cheek.

"Nothing what you up to? Ya girl just squeezed my hand again. I'm still not used to it yet," she said.

"That's a good sign. Hopefully she's closer to waking up."

Lani was about to say something until she seen Candy walk in the room. If looks could kill, that bitch would have dropped dead right on the spot.

"Who are you?" Lani asked.

I jumped up before that bitch could say anything. "Yo what the fuck is you doing? Didn't I tell you to stay yo ass in the car?"

"I already told I was not about to sit in no fucking cold ass car while you sit up in here. I don't know why you here anyways, it ain't like she fucking know you here," Candy said rolling her neck.

I reached back and slapped the shit out of her. Before I even knew what was happening, Lani was running up on her ass. I knew Lani would stomp a hole in Candy's ass so I grabbed her. "Chill Lani."

"Mykell, get this dirty ass bitch out of here. How the fuck you gon bring one of your sluts up here any fucking way?" Lani snapped.

I hurried up and snatched Candy up before a nurse came in. I already knew I was about to catch some flack about this shit once it got back to my pops.

Kamil

It's been six months since I last seen Reneice. I should be happy but I'm not. I really loved that girl. True, I was sent to kill her but being around her so much actually made me fall for her. If I could go back and change everything I would. Honestly, since I left Detroit, I've become somewhat of an alcoholic. I've never been a big drinker but that seems to be all I can do lately.

I guess her family seems to have forgotten about me since no one has come for my head yet. I knew all I had to do was give them some time then everything would die down.

Chapter 4

Ramone

Six damn months later and my sister still laying in that damn hospital bed. Mykell hired a damn private investigator to find out where his hoe ass baby mama and that bitch ass nigga are. Lakey, Howie, Corey and Jason damn near moved up here. They've been here ever since I called them. I knew I had some real niggas on my team. We're all at Mykell's house just chilling and talking shit.

"Man, I'll be happy when Lani have my daughter. Her and them damn weird food cravings she be having starting to get crazy," I said.

"Her ass always been a weird eater," Mack laughed.

"Hell yea, she wouldn't eat macaroni unless it had pickles in it when we were little."

"What the fuck?" Jason laughed.

"That's nothing, she be eating pickles dipped in ice cream and shit." I shook my head.

'I'm happy Neicey never had no weird cravings, her ass was just evil." Mykell laughed.

"I want me some bad ass lil kids running around one day," Mack said out of nowhere.

"What about Tasha? Y'all been hanging pretty tough for the past four months," I inquired.

"Yea but I gotta fill her out some more. I be trynna get Lani to meet her and get her opinion but after that shit Kell pulled, she ain't going," he said referring to Lisa.

"Don't blame that on me."

"It is your fault, you had that girl thinking she was yo girl and she meant something to you." Mack laughed.

"I'm happy I don't have any baby mama drama." Lakey said.

"Shut up," Corey said hitting his brother on the back of the head. "You and Mack the only two niggas here that ain't got no kids."

"I ain't in no rush."

"Being a father is one of the most beautiful things in this world. I wake up every morning, look at MJ and Mell and am proud that I'm a father. Even though that damn Romell got his mama attitude." Everyone laughed.

The laughter came to an end when Mykell's phone rang. "It's the PI."

"Hello?"

He looked at all of us then smiled.

"Okay me and my brothers are on the way now."
He hung up and jumped off the couch. "Let's go y'all. He
said he got something we might want to hear.

* * *

It took us about 30 minutes to get to his office. I
was sitting on pins wondering what information he had
for us.

"Welcome gentlemen," he greeted us.

"What you got for us?" Mykell asked getting
straight to the point.

"I found both of them. I called in a favor from a
friend of mine out in Cali and he tracked your man
down. Also I found your Ms. Olivia Moss but I took me
some pictures just to make sure it was her," he said
sliding Mykell an envelope.

Mykell opened the envelope and looked through
the pictures. "What the fuck!" he suddenly said. That got
everyone's attention.

Mykell

"Ain't this about a bitch?" I said out loud.

"What man?" Mack asked me.

"When was this picture taken?" I held up the
picture so the PI could see.

"Yesterday."

"Okay, thank you," I said going into my pocket and taking out some money, paying for his services.

"Come on y'all," I said getting up.

"Man what you see in them pictures?" Corey asked me.

"We'll talk when we get back to the house."

When we got back to the house, everyone was anxious to hear what I seen in the pictures.

"Okay, I know Mack knows but I'm not sure about the rest of y'all," I took a deep breath. "Before me and Reneice got together, she was messing with a nigga named Quamir. I guess you can say I snatched her and when me and Neicey started going strong, it's like this nigga fell off the face of the earth. Or so I thought."

"So what that nigga go to do with this?" Lakey asked.

"Don't tell me his ass was working with Olivia too?" Mack said.

"Well I guess I don't have to tell you, you just hit it dead on," I confirmed handing him the pictures.

"So one of them muthafuckas must be the one who raped Ladybug," Mone said.

"I'm on the same page as you Mone. My bets are on Q but I still feel some type of way about that nigga Kamil," I agreed.

"Let me see them pictures so I can see what this nigga look like," Corey said.

"Me too, Ladybug never said nothing bout this Q nigga to me."

"Word?" Mack asked shocked.

"Hell naw! And I know about every nigga she's ever dealt with, even when she tried to keep it a secret, but this Q is a mystery to me."

"Well I wanna stake out and watch where these dumb muthafuckas be at. See what else I can find out before we make our move."

Everyone agreed. This shit was getting even crazier. This nigga that I was supposed to be cool with did some foul shit to my girl, but for what though?

Lani

"Mone, bring me some chocolate syrup. Please."

I was having another weird ass craving. We're supposed to be on our way to the hospital to see Neicey but I keep having the urge to pee every five minutes.

"You and these craving are driving me crazy. I'll be happy when you go back to eating normal."

I wanted to reply with a real smart ass comment but I couldn't, I was stuck. *It couldn't be.*

"What's wrong baby?" he asked concerned.

I looked down and he must have followed my eyes and seen the big wet spot.

"Oh shit! It's time!" he yelled.

"Call the doctor while I change my clothes. Luckily I'm not in any pain right now," I said walking into the closet to find some sweat pants to change into.

"They said to bring you in when your contractions are five minutes apart."

"Why are you so calm? You act like you've done this before," I said with a questioning look.

He laughed. "Chill, I was only eight years old when I seen Ladybug born, so I know what to expect."

"Well . . . AHHHH!" I held my stomach and leant over in pain.

"Yo ass having contractions now huh?" Ramone laughed like this shit was funny.

"We are NEVER having sex ever again."

"Whatever man. Imma grab the bag so we can be ready to go."

Twenty minutes later I was laying in the hospital bed feeling like my insides were about to fall out.

"I can't do this shit. This look worse than it did the first time I seen it happen," Ramone said looking like he was about to pass out.

"Nigga please! You did this shit so you better suck it the fuck up and stay yo black ass right here," I said through gritted teeth.

"Okay, Ms. Jones. You are fully dilated so now it's time to push."

I did three big pushes but it seemed like she didn't want to come out. "Somebody get this baby out of me!" I yelled out in pain. This shit was the worst pain ever.

"Alright, I see the head. One more big push for me."

I pushed one more time and it felt like this little girl had ripped me a new asshole. I was overjoyed when I heard my baby cry, it was like music to my ears. I thought I was done but they told me I had to push the afterbirth out. Ramone followed the nurses when they took our daughter to be cleaned off. I was feeling tired as hell.

"Who knew I could create something so beautiful?" Ramone beamed like a proud father when he walked back over to me, kissing me on the forehead.

"She is beautiful. Welcome to the world Ranyla Love Peake," I said to my baby when they put her on my chest.

"Is she alright doc? Why she look like that?" Ramone asked sounding worried.

"She's just tired. Having a baby can be very tiresome and her body went through some traumatic pain but I can assure you that she is alright."

Everyone walked into the room with all types of balloons and teddy bears.

"I need for y'all to stop making me a grandpa, I'm too young for all this," my daddy joked.

"Who you telling? I have more grandkids than I do gray hairs," Poppa Mone laughed.

"Well at least we have another girl in the family. We men were starting to take over," Mack said looking at Ranyla.

"I'm a proud uncle, I have me a little girl to spoil. She kind of looks like Neicey." Mykell chimed in.

"Sorry to interrupt this happy moment," Neicey's doctor said walking into the room and I feared the worst. "I just wanted to inform you all that Ms. Peake is woke," he said smiling.

"Oh my gosh! I have to go see her. I need to take Ranyla to go see her auntie," I said trying to get out the bed even though I was tired as hell.

"Whoa little lady, you stay right there in that bed. We'll all go see her but you need to be in a wheelchair," my daddy said.

"Well tell them to get the chair ready so we can go!" I fussed.

I knew my sister wouldn't let me down. She came back the day her niece was born, just like I asked her to.

Reneice

I opened my eyes and it took me some time to realize where I was. I don't even know how I got to the hospital. I tried to pull that damn tube out of my mouth but it wouldn't budge. I pressed the button to call the nurse and she came in to see me. She was happy to see that I was woke and wasted no time calling the doctor. When they removed the tube a whole lot of gook came up with it but the doctor told me that was normal.

"H-h-h-h-" I tired talking but nothing was coming out like I wanted it to plus my throat was sore as hell.

"Shhh. Don't try to talk sweetie," the Doctor said. "Give your throat a rest and I'll answer any question you want me to when you feel better. Let me call your family.

"You were quite the trooper though," a nurse said.

I felt a pain in my chest on the left side. I put my hand up there and I felt a bandage.

"No worries sweetie, that's where you go shot. I already changed your bandage, if you take care of it right, it will heal right," the nurse said.

I just nodded my head since I couldn't talk.

"Ma! You're up!" MJ yelled running in the room right to my bed.

I kissed him all over his face.

I smiled so hard when I saw the rest of my family enter the room. Lani was wheeled in by Ramon and she had a baby wrapped up in her arms. I couldn't wait to see her.

"L-I-I" I tried to talk again, but all I heard was a weird noise.

"She's cute, huh?" MJ asked.

I shook my head yes. She's actually beautiful, she looks just like Ramone. She has his color and everything. They did real good with her.

"I'm so happy you came back Neicey. You just don't know. I got two blessings in one day," she said placing my niece in my arms. "She looks just like Mone."

Ramone was at the foot of the bed smiling proudly.

I looked up when I saw my dad walk in the room with Romell on his hip. I felt tears falling from my eyes when I saw how big my Fat Man has got. *I wonder if he remembers me.*

"Mama!" he reached for me.

I smiled happy that he remembered who I was. As I looked around, I was happy to see all the people I loved. I don't know how long I've been here but I'm so happy to be back.

Chapter 5

Lakey

Snook been home from the hospital about two months now. We've been keeping in touch since she's been out. She called me up and said she had something important that she wanted to holla at me about.

"Wassup Snook?" I said when she answered the door. "Where Kell?"

"He's took the boys out somewhere."

"Cool, what did you want to talk to me about?"

"I know y'all making a move tonight and I want in on it," she said with a straight face.

"What you talking about?" I asked playing dumb.

"Don't play with me Lashaun. I know y'all been watching Mykell's baby mama waiting to make a move on her ass. I also know that y'all plan on making that move tonight. I'm coming to you because we been partners in crime since we were little. You know what I'm capable of more than any of them. This shit is more personal for me because this bitch that I don't even know, took it upon herself to hire a muthafucka to kill me. Now, are you letting me roll with you or am I going to have to do this shit on my own?"

I just sat there stuck for a minute. She was right though, I do know what she is capable of because I was the one who taught her how to shoot a damn gun and she been a beast ever since.

"Aight, be ready at 12:00 midnight. Not 12:01, not 12:05. 12:00." I sighed. "Mone is going to kill me."

She jumped up, hugged me and kissed me on my cheek. "I knew I could count on you. And don't worry about Mone, I can handle him."

I just shook my head. This girl is as classy as she wanna be but she got a deadly side to her too. We created a monster.

Mykell

"Did you drop the boys off at Pop-Pop's?" Neicey asked plopping down on the bed next to me.

"Yea, they didn't want to go but I took em anyways."

The day Neicey came home from the hospital, she came home with me. I was happy at first but now I don't know. She's here but not like I want her to be. She sleeps in the guest bedroom, she won't let me touch her. I don't know what to call our relationship, if that's even what this is.

"What you getting into tonight?" she asked taking the remote out my hands.

"Hanging with the boys," I halfway lied. I'll be with the boys but we'll be doing more than hanging. "What you bout to do?"

"I got a date," she said smiling.

I don't know if she was saying that shit to fuck with me or if she was serious. Either way I don't approve.

"What the fuck you mean you got a date? With who?"

"Mind yo own business," she said before her phone rang. She looked at it and smiled before she got of the bed to leave the room.

I sat there feeling some type of way. I know before everything went down we weren't together but when she came home with me, I thought that meant she wanted to work on our relationship. *Enough of this bullshit, we need to talk.* I got up to find her, I walked past the guest bedroom but stopped in my tracks when I heard her laughing.

The door was closed so I got closer so I could hear better.

"I already told you I'll be ready. You don't need to worry about him, I'll handle him."

It got quiet for a minute, then I heard her speak again.

"I can't wait! I'll see you when you get here."

I took that as my cue to go in. When I opened the door she was getting undressed. Since she was in a coma for six months she lost a lot of weight. But her ass was still fat.

"Are you going to stare at me all night or are you going to tell me what you want?"

"We need to talk."

"About?"

"Us."

"Ain't nothing changed Kell, we're still not together," she said, going into the bathroom and closing the door.

Well damn, aight.

*   *   *

I pulled up to the old warehouse I used to use to handle business when I was in the game. I saw everyone's car and was happy that they were on time. I walked in and saw that somebody had already went to work on Q. His face was bloody and swollen, but I guess nobody wanted to touch Olivia because she looked perfectly fine besides the fact that she was tied to a chair.

I looked around and noticed Lakey was missing. "Where the fuck is Lakey?"

"He said he was going to be a little late," Corey spoke up for his brother.

"Well, well, well. Look at what we got here," I said pacing in front of the duo.

"So I guess you bitches thought you had got away with the bullshit you pulled huh?" I stopped in front of Olivia. "Well think again muthafuckas."

The door opened and in walked Lakey.

"Fuck you Mykell. All this shit is your fault," Olivia said with an attitude.

"How so?" I asked confused.

"If you would have just left that bitch Kya alone like I asked you to and been a family with me and your son, I would have never had to call the police on yo dumb ass," she said throwing me off guard.

She laughed. "Yea nigga, I was the one who told the police about the drugs. Too bad you didn't go through with the shipment like you were supposed to because then yo ass would still be locked up and not trynna play house with the next bitch. You were supposed to be with me not anybody else!"

If I had known this bitch was this crazy a long time ago, I never would have fucked with her ass.

I was shook out of my thoughts by Olivia's kneecap damn near being blown off and her loud ass scream. I turned around to see who did it.

"What the fuck?" I yelled.

Reneice

"I know y'all niggas didn't think y'all was gon have all the fun did you?" I smiled devilishly.

I walked up to Mykell and kissed him. "We'll talk later." I was having a damn adrenalin rush from this shit.

"Now bitch, that pain ain't shit compared to the pain you caused me. You had me raped, beaten, killed my unborn child, had *my* son kidnapped, had my house shot up with me and my baby in it. All for what though?"

"YOU HAD MY MAN!" she yelled.

I was getting tired of this bullshit so I shot her in the other knee. "Bitch, he was never yours to begin with. You were just the dumb sidebitch that got caught in her feelings and ended up pregnant. That don't make him yours sweetie." I laughed.

"You sure know how to pick em huh?" I asked Mykell sarcastically.

"Fuck you bitch, he treated yo ass like he treated all the rest of us. You don't mean shit to him just like I didn't."

"Maybe you're right," I shot her in the head.

I walked over to Q. "So yo limp dick ass like raping women huh?"

I sat on Q's lap. "Why'd you do it Quamir? The fuck have I ever done that was so bad you had to rape me?"

"You said fuck me when that nigga came home. We were supposed to be together but the moment he laid his wack ass game down, you said fuck me."

I got up and shook my head at him. "So since you couldn't get the pussy, you had to take it huh?"

"Yea and it was worth it too." He smirked through swollen lips.

Ramone punched him in his mouth and pulled his gun out from behind his back.

"Stop, Mone. I got this," I said before shooting Q in his dick.

"Y'all can do whatever the fuck y'all want with them now. Play time for Neicey is over," I said walking towards the door. "I need a fucking cigarette."

Mykell

"Finish this shit up! Do whatever y'all want with these niggas."

To say I was pissed would be a damn understatement. Who the fuck told Neicey to show her lil ass up? How the fuck did she even know what the fuck was going down?

I walked out into the cool night air mad as fuck looking for her. I saw her leaning up against my truck.

"What the fuck was that shit?" I asked yanking her by her arm.

She looked at my hand on her arm then looked up at me.

"You got one second to release my fucking arm or that ass will be in there stanking with the other two," she said, blowing smoke in my face.

"So you think you just gangster all of a sudden, huh? And when the fuck did you start smoking?"

"I'm 22 damn years old. I don't have to explain shit I do, especially to yo ass."

"You know I'm getting real tired of yo smart ass mouth and fucked up attitude," I said walking closer up on her. Not giving a fuck that the rest of the guys were coming out and setting the building on fire.

"I don't give a fuck!" she spat.

"Get yo ass in the truck before you make me have to beat yo ass out here," I said opening the door and pushing her ass in the passenger's seat.

We argued all the way home. I don't know what the fuck was up with her damn attitude but I know it was pissing me off.

"What the fuck is your problem yo?"

"Nothing Mykell. I just want to go to bed, I'm tired of arguing," she said walking up the stairs.

This girl gon make me put my hands on her. I took a deep breath and went up to my room, grabbed a pre-rolled blunt off my dresser and lit it up. I only took three tokes before I put it out and jumped in the shower.

When I got out the shower, Neicey was laying in my bed with one of my t-shirts on. I just shook my head at this crazy ass girl.

"Why you in my bed with my shirt on?" I asked putting on some boxers.

"Shut up. I already told you I'm done arguing with you."

I just climbed in bed and she snuggled up to me. She had her ass pressed up against my dick. *She wanna fucking play.* I put my hand under her shirt and saw she didn't have any panties on.

She opened her legs and gave me more access. "If you wanted some dick that's all yo ass had to say instead of throwing a damn temper tantrum."

She rolled over on her back and I climbed on top of her. I tried to scoot down but she stopped me.

"Fuck all that, just fuck me."

I had no choice but to oblige her request. I climbed back up her body and put my dick at her opening. I put it in and she gasped. I know it's been a while for her and I could tell because her shit was as tight as it was the night I took her virginity.

"I'm happy you decided to come back to daddy," I said while pumping.

"Shut up and fuck me."

We went at it all night in every position we could think of. It felt good being back up in that, so good that it put a nigga right to sleep.

Chapter 6

Lani

It's been too long since me and Neicey hung out so it was only right that we got together. I sat back and watched as she played with Ranyla.

"Hey TT baby. Hey mamas!"

"Y'all are too cute." I laughed at the funny faces they were making.

"Girl, I miss when Romell was this little."

"You might as well have another one then. Kell been talking about wanting a little girl to spoil," I informed her.

"I'll pass, besides me and your brother ain't even rocking like that."

"So y'all not together?" I asked for conformation.

"No mami, ain't nothing changed."

"Good, so let me tell you what his black ass did," I said ready to tell it all. "He brought some bitch up to the hospital one day while you was in a coma. Don't worry though, I dead that shit before it could even start."

"Say what now?" she asked.

"Yes girl, I put that bitch out the room so fast and told him to follow the bitch after I bit into his ass."

"Damn, I wish you would have told me that before I had a weak moment," she said rocking Ranyla to sleep.

"You didn't," I laughed.

"Girl, I was horny. It's been what? Seven months since I had some dick, I had to have some. At least I put it on him good because he won't be getting it no more."

I just shook my head, this girl is a hot mess.

"Ramone!" she called out.

"What big head!"

"Watch Ny Ny, we'll be back."

"Where we going?"

"Where y'all going?" Ramone asked coming into the den.

"Out, now mind yo business," she said grabbing my hand and pulling me off the couch.

* * *

We were out having drinks when we were approached by two very delicious looking men.

"Hello ladies, sorry to interrupt but I just had to come over and say that you are the two most beautiful women we have ever seen," the dark one said eyeing Neicey.

"Thank you, we really appreciate it."

"No problem. I'm Marco and this is my cousin Zamier."

"I'm Le'Lani and this is my sister Reneice."

"You can call me Neicey," Neicey said speaking up.

Looking at these two gorgeous men almost made me forget that I have a man at home. We're only having a harmless conversation, there's nothing wrong with that.

"Do you mind if we join you?" Zamier asked.

"No, we don't mind at all," Neicey said while winking at me.

I just shook my head, *this girl is going to get me in trouble.*

Reneice

I instantly wet my panties when I laid eyes on Marco. He's tall darn and sexy, just how I like em. The fact that he has grey eyes was an added bonus. I'm guessing he was about 6'2 with muscles out of this world, the V-neck he had on left nothing to the imagination. His goatee was on point right along with his low cut Caesar that would make you seasick if you looked at them for too long.

"So Reneice—"

"Call me Neicey," I interrupted.

"Neicey, are you single?"

"Yes but my situation is a little messed up." I shook my head remembering I had not one but two ex-fiancés that fucked me over and turned out not to be shit.

"How so?" He asked.

"Maybe I'll tell you one day. I don't want to scare you away," I half joked.

"Fair enough."

"So where did you get those pretty eyes from?" I asked.

"Good question. I'm the only one with them in my family." He smiled showing off a pretty set of 32's.

"So Miss Neicey, do you mind if I ask for your number?"

"Only if you really plan on using it." I smiled.

"Oh, trust me I will dimples."

We exchanged numbers and went our separate ways shortly after.

                    *   *   *

After I dropped Lani off, I went to pick up my babies. I was told while I was in the hospital MJ was getting suspended from school for fighting. I'm not surprised though, he has his father's temper. The older he gets, the more he starts to act like and look like Mykell. Sad to say but Romell does too, they're both splitting images of their dad.

"Ma, are you cooking or do I have to eat McDonald's?" MJ asked.

"If you dad hasn't cooked already I'll do it."

"Yayyy! Mommy cook," Romell yelled.

I looked in the rearview mirror and smiled. My baby was almost two years old and damn near speaking in perfect sentences.

When we got to the house, the boys took off running towards their rooms.

"What I tell y'all about running in the house!" I yelled only for it to fall on deaf ears.

"Leave my sons alone," Mykell said coming down the stairs.

I rolled my eyes, "How about I leave you and *your* sons here while I go on a vacation," I said, sitting on the couch.

"Or we could just take a vacation as a family," Mykell said putting my feet on his lap and massaging them.

"I guess we could make that happen."

"We *should* make that happen." He moved his hand higher up my leg until he reached my belt buckle. Everything that Lani had told me about him having another bitch at the hospital came back to me.

I grabbed his hand and stopped him. "What? Wassup?" he asked like he was irritated.

"I can't go there with you."

"Why not?"

"Mommy, MJ won't let me play the game," Romell said scaring the hell out of me.

"Okay baby, here I come." I jumped off the couch, happy that he interrupted.

Mykell

See that's that crazy shit I be talking about. One minute she fucking my brains out then the next minute she act like she don't wanna be bothered.

I heard a phone vibrating and knew it wasn't mines. I wasn't going to answer her phone until I seen she had text message from Marco.

Who the fuck is Marco? I thought as I clicked on the message.

Hello Dimples, I just wanted to tell you I had a great time with you today and I hope it won't be the last time. Let me know the next time you're available so I can take you out. Stay beautiful.

"What the fuck?" I kept looking at the message. "Neicey!" I yelled.

"What? Why you yelling?" she asked coming down the stairs.

"Who the fuck is Marco?"

"Huh?"

"If you ass can huh I'm pretty sure you can fucking hear. Who is Marco?" I asked again.

"Nobody you need to be worried about," she sassed with her hands on her hips.

"Don't fuckin play with me Reneice. Who is this nigga? I thought you said you was with Lani today."

"First of all, you not my daddy nor my nigga so I don't have to answer a damn thing." She rolled her neck. "Not once did I ask you who was the bitch you brought up to the hospital so therefore don't question shit I do. I'm a grown ass woman." She snatched her phone out my hand.

Imma kick Le'Lani's ass! She just couldn't wait to run her fucking mouth.

I didn't intentionally bring another bitch to the hospital. I told her to stay her ass in the car but she was too fucking hardheaded and nosey, she just had to hop her happy ass out the car. Lani shut that shit down before it could even start so I don't know why she felt the need to tell Neicey shit.

Micah

Everyone else around me was all booed up with kids. I just laid back and watched all the issues they had in their relationships and it almost made me wanna stay single forever. All that changed when I met my lil mama, Janae. She's cool, smart, independent, great personality and sexy as hell. I've been trying to get Lani to meet up with us so she can meet Janae but she wasn't trying to hear it after that shit Kell pulled with Lisa. My sister could always tell when a female wasn't right for me or Kell and ten times out of ten, she was right.

I remembered the day I met Janae.

MJ's school was going on a fieldtrip to go see the Tigers play baseball. Of course Neicey couldn't go and Mykell wanted to stay with her so I said I would go. MJ wanted to go to the concession stand to get him some nachos, as we headed towards the stands. A little girl bumped into me. She looked like she was only in the first grade.

"I can't find my mommy," she said with tears in her eyes.

I got some money out my pocket and told MJ to go get whatever he wanted while I helped the little girl find her mom.

"Thanks unc," he said walking away.

"Okay sweetie, what's your name?" I asked picking her up.

"Ranee."

"Alright Ranee I'm Micah. Do you remember what color your mommy had on?"

"Red."

"Alright, let's see if we can find her."

We walked around for five minutes looking for her mom but we had no luck.

"Ranee!" I heard somebody calling from behind me. I turned to see a lady looking like she was about to cry. I knew it had to be her mother because she was wearing red but I asked her anyways just to make sure.

"Ranee, is that your mommy?" I asked pointing to the lady.

"Yes!" she said excitedly.

I walked towards the lady. "Excuse me miss, your daughter has been looking for you."

I was taken aback by her beauty. She didn't have any makeup or anything on but she was still beautiful. She couldn't be any taller than 5'4, pretty brown eyes with long eyelashes.

"Oh my god! Thank you so much," she said as I handed Ranee over.

"Thank you Mr. Micah," Ranee said.

"No problem sweetie, in big places like this you have to stay close to your mommy."

"Okay," she said.

Her mother reached her hand out for me to shake. "I'm Janae."

"Micah," I said shaking her hand. When I did that, I felt sparks fly.

"I can't thank you enough. You just don't know how scared I was."

"No problem, I would do it for anybody."

That day we exchanged numbers and we've been close ever since. I can't really explain it, but I really feel something for her.

I talked to Neicey and she agreed to meet her, I know my baby girl would come through for me.

"You nervous?" I asked Janae.

"Nah, I'm good. They can't be that bad."

Shit, you don't know my sisters like that. I thought to myself.

The doorbell rang and I got up to answer it.

"Mack daddy!" Neicey said when I opened the door.

"Wassup thing one and thing two," I joked.

"Hey Mack. Okay, I'm here so let's get down to business," Lani said walking to the den.

Here we go.

"Neicey, Lani, this is Janae. Janae, these are my sisters," I introduced.

"Now that that's out the way," Neicey said. "Mack, Imma need for you to have a seat. This is the Lani and Neicey show now."

I just shook my head and hoped that Janae was ready for whatever they crazy asses were about to throw her way.

"First, I just wanna say that nigga sitting over there," she pointed at me, "he's my heart. Fucking him over is like fucking me over and trust, I'm not the type of bitch you wanna fuck over. You should feel lucky that he even wants us to meet you. Me and Lani are the babies of the family and we go hard for the men in our life. I mean we get down and dirty.... fuck that, we get grimy... we love getting our hands dirty and if you think you're too good for that, you know where the door is."

Neicey sat her ass down on the loveseat like her ass was the damn godfather or something. Then Lani decided to get up.

"Like my lil sister over here already told you, we go hard for the men in our family. Especially since we're the only girls. Now, we've had some bitches and niggas come into our family that wasn't bout shit and we vowed we would never let that shit happen again. Neicey's the type to whoop yo ass the first time then put a bullet in yo ass the second time. Me? I will cut yo ass with a quickness and not think twice about it. All I want to know is can you dig that?"

Janae looked at me then dug into her purse and pulled out a chrome .45 and put it on the coffee table. "Looks like we got two bitches who like to shoot."

Lani smiled. "Anything you wanna say about that Neicey?"

"Yup," she got up and walked to Janae. "Welcome to the family."

My jaw hit the floor. I didn't know Janae was packing but I was happy to know she could hold her own. *There's some shit we gon have to talk about.*

Janae

Meeting Micah was one of the best days of my life. Before I met him, my life was dark and gloomy. I lost my first love Rodney two years ago in a robbery. They killed him then took all his money from him. I was so lost without him. I had went through a real deep depression, at the time I didn't know I was pregnant. I decided that it wasn't about me anymore. I know had a child I had to live for. Ranee is my world, I wouldn't trade her for nothing. I believe Micah was heaven sent.

I told him my whole story and not one time did he judge me. He listened to me, let me cry on his shoulder and wiped my tears away. He told me he would always be there for me no matter what and I believe him. When I'm around, I feel so safe. The feelings that I have for him, I haven't felt for anyone in two years.

It's an added bonus that Ranee loves him too. Whenever he calls, she makes sure that she has her own little conversation with him. He buys her anything she wants. I've never seen a two year old so spoiled. I understand where Neicey and Lani was coming from and I don't blame them for coming at me the way they did. I would have done the same thing but they don't have to worry about me hurting or fucking over Micah. He's one of the best things to ever happen to me since giving birth and I wouldn't mess that up, ever.

Chapter 7

Kamil

It's been a year since I've seen or heard from Neicey. I would be lying if I said I didn't miss her. I know shit seemed a little crazy but I just need her to understand that I never meant for shit to go down the way it did. I really did love her; still do. That's why I didn't do the job, I just couldn't go through with it.

I miss her smell, her touch, the way she felt when I was inside her, hell I just miss her period.

I recently kicked my alcoholism and haven't had a drink in three months but I still feel like shit because I can't get Neicey off my mind.

I just need to hear her voice, let her know how sorry I am.

Fuck it, I thought as I picked up the phone and dialed her number.

Reneice

Marco and I have been on three dates since we've met. Right now we're keeping things on a friendship level, he understands that I'm not trying to rush into anything. I opened up to him and told him everything from my breakup with Mykell to being in a coma. Not one time did he judge me, instead he listened.

Today MJ wanted to have a movie night as a family. I could tell he knew things were different between me and his father and he tried to get us together whenever he could.

We were watching *Iron Man 3* when I got a call from an unknown number. I wasn't going to answer, but I went against my better judgment.

"Hello?" Nobody said anything but I knew somebody was on the line because I could hear them breathing.

"Hello?" I said again.

"Neicey?"

I instantly froze up when I heard that voice. They were talking just above a whisper but I knew exactly who it was.

I could feel Mykell burning a hole in the side of my head so I got up and went upstairs to my bedroom.

"Hello?" Kamil said again.

"Really Kamil? You call my phone after a year like everything is good between us?" I fussed in a low tone just in case Mykell was outside the door eavesdropping.

"Look Neicey, I know I'm probably the last person you want to hear from but I just had to let you know that I never meant to hurt you. Shit wasn't supposed to go down like that, I really do love you. That's why I didn't go through with it and told them to leave you alone, because I loved you. Still do. I really am sorry Neicey," he said sincerely.

"I was in a coma for six fucking months Kamil. Six months! All you can come up with is 'I'm sorry'? If you would have been real with me from jump, none of this shit would have went down. I almost lost my life behind some jealousy bullshit and if you love me like you claim you do, you would have told me."

I was fighting back the tears that were threatening to fall. Kamil really hurt me.

"I really am sorry Reneice. I thought I was protecting you by not telling you. I swear I didn't know you were in the hospital, I never meant for this shit to happen." His voice cracked.

I took a deep breath. "I believe you."

"What? You do?"

There was a knock at the door and I jumped. "Look, I gotta go. It was nice talking to you."

"Can I call you back?"

"I'll call you," I whispered into the phone before I hung up.

I went to the door and unlocked it, when I opened it Mykell was standing there with a strange look on his face.

"What's wrong? Why you crying?"

Shit! I wiped my eyes before I replied. "I'm fine," I said trying to walk around him but he blocked me.

"Don't lie to me Reneice, who called you?"

"Mykell, I'm fine."

What the hell have I gotten myself into?

* * *

I met up with Lani and Janae, we were having a girl's night at Janae's house. Ever since Mack introduced us, we clicked and have been inseparable. I need somebody to talk to about the phone call I received the other day.

"What's on ya mind mami?" Lani asked.

"Okay, I'm about to tell y'all something but you can't tell Ramone or Micah."

"We won't," Lani agreed.

I took a deep breath before I started. "Kamil called me the other day."

"What the fuck! Where was Kell?" Lani asked.

"He was right by me when he called." I shook my head.

"They gon kill him," Janae said.

I already filled her in on the situation so she knows how serious this is.

"So what did he say? What did you say?" Lani asked in one breath.

"Well he apologized and said he never meant for it to go down like that. Talking about he loves me and that's why he never went through with it," I explained.

"If he really loved you like he claims he wouldn't have let that shit go down, period," Lani said.

"I agree, he would have killed both of them bitches if they tried any funny shit. The fact that he knew and you got raped but he *still* never said anything is foul as hell Neicey," said Janae, agreeing with Lani.

I just sat back because I had a lot on my mind. Everything that they were saying is true. *I just don't know what to do.*

Mykell

Things with me and Neicey still weren't where I wanted them to be. It's cool though, I got me a little freak by the name of Candy that I been breaking off lately. I'm not feeling her to the point where I would want to be in a relationship with her, never that. It's just sex, nothing more and I make sure she understands that because I don't want her ass getting confused.

Honestly, she ain't got shit on Neicey, she's nowhere on her level. I find myself comparing females to Neicey a lot. That shit just comes natural. I was at home waiting for Neicey and the boys to get back home. It seems like ever since she has been home from the hospital, they have been stuck to her like glue. I was about to fix me something to eat but my phone rang and caught my attention. *What she want?* I thought before I answered.

"Yo!"

"Hey daddy," Candy cooed into the phone.

"Wassup?"

"You coming through tonight?"

"I don't know about that"

She sucked her teeth. "Why not?"

"Yo don't be questioning me, I already told yo ass I'm not coming!"

Right when I said that, Neicey and the boys walked through the door.

"Imma call you back man." I hung up without waiting for a response.

"You don't have to rush off the phone when I walk in the room," Neicey said giving me the side eye.

"Whatever man."

"Anyways, I'm leaving the boys here with you tonight so I hope you don't have any plans."

"Actually I do. You always wanna go out somewhere, stay yo ass home sometimes."

"I haven't been out in a while. I'm just going out with Lani and Janae for a dinner date. Besides, I don't need your permission to do a damn thing," she said, getting up and walking away.

Her ass and that damn smart mouth.

Chapter 8

Lakey

It's been a while since me and Reneice kicked it so I thought I would see what was up with her and baby Mell. I was too happy when she asked me to be his godfather, that's my little man. He look like Kell but act like Neicey, a deadly combination.

I got some news to drop on her and I don't know how she gon take it but I'd rather her hear it from me then somebody else.

"Hey big head! I missed you," she said when she got in my car.

"Wassup knucklehead." I laughed then looked in the backset at Romell. "Wassup lil man?"

"Wassup!" he said excitedly.

"He getting so big man, damn." I shook my head.

"I know right. But what you been up to stranger? You must got a girl now, that's the only time you act funny towards me." She chuckled.

"Says the girl who ran away and left me to start her own family." I playfully mushed her head.

"Hey don't touch my mommy!" Romell fussed.

"That's right baby, get him." She stuck her tongue out at me.

"Naw but for real, I wanna run something by you." I said getting serious.

"Hit me with it then."

"I'm moving to Florida next week. It's big things popping down there and I think that's the best move for me to make."

I waited for her response but never got one. She just looked straight ahead.

"Yo, what's on yo mind Snook? Say something."

She turned and looked at me. "Sooo when can me and Fat Fat come to visit?" She cracked a smile that I could tell was fake.

"Whenever y'all want."

"Cool, now let's go." She turned and looked out the window.

The rest of the day was awkward between me and Neicey. She seemed to be a little more distant. *What the fuck is up with her?*

Ramone

Things have been real hectic for me lately. For some reason I feel like I'm living a double life, not intentionally but that's just the way it is. Carmen is a chick I was messing with before Le'Lani. She tried to tell me that she was pregnant with my baby but I stopped fucking with her because I wasn't ready for any kids at the time. The only person that knew about the situation was Neicey, I'm not sure if she told Lani or not being that they tell each other everything.

Now Carmen is calling my phone constantly bashing me for not spending anytime with my son. I never got a blood test or nothing so I'm not really sure if he's my son or not. He looks just like Carmen. If he does turn out to be mine, I'll feel bad about missing out on three years of his life.

How am I going to tell Le'Lani? How will she feel about it? Will she try to leave me?

I was shook out my thoughts by the ringing of my phone.

"Hello?"

"Are you coming to see your son today or what?"

"Man, I just seen him yesterday."

"So the fuck what! You see that bitch's daughter every day, why can't you see my son every day? Besides I think he needs to meet his little sister."

"When we get a blood test and he is proven to be mine, then I'll let him meet her."

"I bet you didn't ask her to have a blood test, you know what Ramone? You're full of shit!" she said before I heard the line go dead.

I just sat back on the couch and sighed deeply. One minute I was living the picture perfect life with the girl of my dreams now shit was going from sweet to sour.

I need to talk to my dad and Pop-Pop about this one.

* * *

Last week I took my dad and Pop-Pop's advice. They told me to just get the DNA test done and let Lani know so there won't be any more surprises. Well, I did one but I still can't seem to tell Lani.

Now I'm stuck as hell sitting here looking at the paper that tells me that I am 99.9% the father of Keiyari Ramone Peake. *Damn, this is fucked up.*

Lani

Today is the day of my baby's first birthday. To say that I am excited is an understatement. Me, Neicey and Janae went shopping and got princess everything for Ranyla's birthday. We went crazy with the shopping. It's going to be so much fun. Of course daddy wants the party to be at his house, like always.

It's pink and white balloons everywhere. The men were help setting up the rest of the decorations while the ladies were in the kitchen finishing up the food. Even little Ranee was being a good little helper.

There was a knock at the door. "I'll get it," I said since I was the closet to it.

I opened the door to find a woman holding a very handsome little boy. I'm guessing he was her son.

"Hi can I help you?" I asked.

"You must be Lani. Is Ramone here?" she said with an attitude.

"Hold on please."

What the fuck? Who is this bitch?

"Neicey! Janae!" I yelled walking back into the kitchen.

"What girl? What's wrong?" Janae asked.

"Some bitch with a child is at the door asking for Ramone," I said.

Neicey wasted no time getting up and running to the door. Janae and I were right on her heels.

"May I ask what you want with Ramone?" Neicey asked nicely.

"His son needs to meet his sister." She replied.

"Hold up, did you say son?" I asked.

"Yes, my son and your daughter are brother and sister."

"And your name is?" Janae spoke up.

"Carmen. Look can ya'll please just go get Ramone."

Imma kill this nigga. On my mama, Imma kill him.

"How about you just come with us in the back to get him," I said

"Great idea," she said smartly.

Don't cut this bitch Lani, it's about your daughter today, I said to myself.

When we got outside, the men were laughing and joking around. I was about to put a stop to all that shit.

I cleared my throat and got their attention. When Ramone noticed Carmen, he turned as white as a ghost.

"Hey guys, I want you to meet Carmen. Ramone's baby mama, and his son. What's your son's name Ramone?" I asked trying not to lose my cool.

He just stood there looking stupid. All eyes were on him.

"Oh you can't answer me?"

"Keiyari," he said in a low tone.

"Right," I turned to Carmen and Keiyari. "Well you two have a seat. I have some business I need to tend too," I said walking away before the tears could fall.

"Baby!"

"No Mone, you stay here. I got her," I heard Neicey say.

It felt like my world just came crashing down.

Reneice

Too much bullshit has been going on lately. It seems like everything that could go wrong, did go wrong. I can't believe that Mone would keep some shit like that from us. From my understanding, he said he found out the baby wasn't his. I feel just as betrayed as Lani. He has never lied to me before so I'm confused as to why he felt the need to do it now.

I invited Lani and Janae to come out to eat with me. Lani has been sitting up in the house ever since she found out about Ramone's son. She hasn't been home since either, she's been staying with Pop-Pop and I can't say that I blame her.

Janae and I were doing our best to lift Lani's spirits when I looked up and saw Marco. He was looking too fine for words. He smiled when his eyes met mine. He walked in with his cousin Zamier and another one of his homeboys.

"Hey beautiful, what you been up to besides dodging me?" he asked giving me a hug.

"I was not dodging you. I had a lot going on that was taking up my free time," I said hugging him back." I looked at Zamier and spoke to him.

"Would you fellas like to join us?" I asked.

"Sure, why not," Marco agreed.

Zamier sat down by Lani and must have sensed something was wrong with her. "What's the matter pretty lady?"

"I just have lot on my mind."

"Oh yea?" he asked before leaning over and whispering something in her ear.

She smiled before she busted out laughing.

I was happy to see her get out of the funk she was in. The next thing I know, I was being pulled up out the chair by my hair.

"WHAT THE FUCK!" I yelled.

I saw Marco, Zamier and their homie jump up.

"What the fuck is you doing in here smiling all up in this nigga face?" Mykell asked still holding a tight grip on my hair.

"Mykell let her go! What the fuck is wrong with you?" Lani asked.

"Mykell, you got ten seconds to let go of my hair or we gon fuck this restaurant up," I said through gritted teeth.

"Mykell who is this?" some ratchet looking bitch asked.

Mykell ignored her and dragged me outside, still holding me by my hair.

"You fucking that nigga?" he asked finally letting me go and throwing me up against his truck.

I reared back and slapped this shit out of him with all my might.

"You must have lost yo damn mind! Don't be putting yo hands on me like that."

"Answer my fucking question Reneice. Are you fucking that nigga?" he said walking closer to me. At that moment I could smell the alcohol on his breath.

"How many times do I have to tell you, I'm grown as fuck? I don't answer to you or nan other nigga."

"Well miss grown as fuck, how about you get yo shit out my house and let that nigga take care of you then," he said walking away with his bitch behind him.

Everybody else came out the restaurant to check on me and make sure I was okay.

* * *

The next morning I woke up with a horrible headache. I swear it felt like Mykell was trying to detach my hair from my scalp. I looked over and noticed Lani laying in the bed with me. We had a real serious sister to sister moment last night.

I did a lot of thinking and thought it was best that I get my stuff out of Mykell's house. Pop-Pop said I can stay with him for however long I wanted but it would be too easy for Mykell to drop his ass by at any time.

I made a decision to go stay with my dad. He lived far enough away from everybody so I could just have some time to myself to think.

I pulled up to Mykell's house hopping he wasn't here so I could just get in, get my son and my belongings, and then get out. Simple as that. I walked into the house and went straight to my son's room. He was sitting on his bed watching SpongeBob.

"Hey Fat Fat," I spoke grabbing his attention.

"Mommy!" he yelled excitedly.

"Hey baby, how are you?"

"Fine, I watch SpongeBob mommy." He pointed to the TV.

"I see."

"What's up with all the noise little man?" I heard from behind me and was face to face with the bitch Mykell was with last night. She had on one of Mykell's t-shirts with nothing else on.

"Bitch you need to put some clothes on when yo ass is around my son!" I yelled.

I just know this nigga didn't have this nasty looking bitch around my son, I just know he didn't.

"What's up with all this damn yelling?" Mykell asked walking in the room rubbing his eyes.

He froze when he seen me. "N-Neicey, what you doing here?"

"Really Mykell? While my son was here? Really, that's how we doing it now?"

I didn't even give him time to speak. I picked Romell up and walked right out the room.

"Neicey, wait let me explain. It wasn't even like that."

"Mykell you don't have to explain shit to her, she not yo woman," this bitch had the nerve to say.

I stopped dead in my tracks. "On the strength of my son being here is the only reason why I'm not gon tap yo ass or put a bullet in you," I said before walking right out the door ignoring Mykell's begging and pleading.

I buckled my son is his seat then hurried up and hopped in the front seat and sped out of his driveway. "Bye daddy!" Romell yelled while waving.

I don't care that he has another female, I just felt disrespected that he would be fucking another female while my son was in the house. Fuck those clothes and shoes at the house, I don't care what he do with them. My son and I will be starting over fresh.

Chapter 9

Mykell

It's been almost a months since I've seen Neicey or my son. I understand that she was mad but to keep my son from me is some bullshit. No matter what we went through she always allowed me to see him, now she on some other shit. I can't even get a phone call letting me know that they still alive or something. What type of shit is that?

Mone told me that she been spending a lot of time with that bitch ass nigga I seen her with. You would think after all the bullshit she went through with Kamil, she would sit the fuck down somewhere. Ever since she woke up from that coma, she been acting real funny. I got a feeling that she might be fucking that nigga too, she wasn't giving it to me so she had to be giving it to somebody.

"Dad, what did you do to my mom?" MJ asked with a mug on his face.

I looked at his little ass like he was crazy. "What makes you think I did something to her?"

"Because you're always doing something to make her mad. I haven't seen her and Fat Fat in forever and it's all your fault."

I just sat there and looked at my son. His ass was 11 going on 30. "MJ, go sit ya lil ass down somewhere okay? Stay out of grown folks business you don't even know what you talking about."

"Pop-Pop was right, you and uncle Mone are pushing the ladies away. Uncle Mack will be the only one who lives happily ever after," he said before heading towards the stairs.

Imma end up beating his lil ass. I thought about what he said, I'm not pushing Neicey away. She's pushing her own self away.

*   *   *

Since Neicey been on her lil bullshit, I been keeping Candy's dumb ass real close. I have to keep reminding her that she is not wifey. I'm not the type of nigga to lead a female on, Imma tell you what I want and either you with it or you not.

"Yo man, chill on all that attitude shit. I'm not in the mood for all that."

"Mykell, I'm sick of this shit, every time her ass do something to make you mad, you get a funky ass attitude with me."

"I got a damn attitude because yo ass wanna nag a nigga to death. How bout you shut the fuck up and put something in yo mouth," I said before I took a toke on the blunt I was smoking.

"Ugh, I can't stand you!" she stumped off like a little ass kid.

Immature ass, that's some shit MJ would do.

I was about to lay back and close my eyes until my phone rang. I looked it and it was Micah.

"Wassup nigga?"

"Man, you need to get to the hospital like yesterday."

I sat up on the couch, "Why, wassup man?"

"It's Romell. I'll tell you everything, just get here man!" he yelled before hanging up.

What the fuck is really good?

Reneice

I was at the park with Marco and Romell. Lately Marco has become a real good friend, he understands that I'm not trying to get into another relationship anytime soon. I was laughing at something that Marco said when I heard a loud scream. I turned around and noticed Romell was in the parking lot with a car speeding in his direction.

"MY BABY!" I screamed.

Marco ran towards him to try to save him but it was too late. The car hit Romell. He flew in the air and hit the ground hard. I let out a gut wrenching scream that even I didn't recognize. I was stuck, I couldn't move. It felt like my legs had suddenly been paralyzed. Marco swooped Romell up in his arms and ran to the car. I still couldn't move.

"Come on Neicey, we have to get him to the hospital." I heard Marco say.

I still didn't move. He came and carried me to the car.

"I know you're in shock but I need you to call his dad," Marco said speeding and damn near breaking every traffic law.

My hands shook while I dialed Pop-Pop's number. "Wassup baby girl?" he answered.

"I...I...I'm sorry." I broke down.

"What's wrong Neicey, talk to me baby girl."

"I..."

Marco took the phone from me and told Pop-Pop everything. When we got to the hospital, Marco jumped out the car and ran inside. He came back out with nurses. They took my baby and put him on a gurney.

Marco helped me out the car and led me to the waiting room. My nerves were all over the place. Romell had been back there for twenty minutes and they still haven't came and told us nothing. I sat there rocking back and forth. "Please don't let my baby die," I keep saying.

Lani, Janae, Micah, Ramone, Pop-Pop and my dad all came running to me.

"Ladybug, talk to me. What happened?"

I just looked at him. I haven't felt like this since I was beat, raped and lost my first baby. *It's happening again. Why is God punishing me?*

Marco rubbed my back and told them everything that happened.

I seen Mykell come in, and what do you know, he had his bitch with him.

"What the fuck is she doing here?" Janae asked getting everyone's attention.

"Really Mykell?" Lani asked.

Mykell ignored them and came straight to me. "What the fuck happened Reneice?"

Before I could respond, the doctor came out. "Well he has a couple of broken bones, fractured ribs and when he hit the ground, he hit his head real hard. It caused his brain to swell so we want to keep him here until we can get some of the swelling to go down. I already put a cast on his arm and I gave him something for the pain so he'll be out of it."

I felt myself falling but before I could hit the ground, Marco caught me.

He walked me back to my seat. "It's going to be okay sweetie, if he's anything like you, I know he's a fighter and he'll be alright," he tried to assure me.

Mykell stormed over to me. "See Reneice, you doing all that hoeing around and look what happened. All because you can't keep yo fucking legs closed, my son in there and almost lost his fucking life!"

"That's enough Mykell!" Pop-Pop said.

Mykell ignored him and kept going. "Some shit always going down because you following up behind some dick! Ain't shit go wrong in this family until I met yo trifling ass," he spat before walking off.

I would be lying if I said his words didn't sting, actually they hurt like hell. Here was the man that I once loved more than anything talking to me like I didn't mean shit to him. *Fuck him, I'm worried about my son. He can go to hell for all I care.*

"Let me go handle this nigga," Pop-Pop said walking off.

"Let him go Pop-Pop," I said.

"Fuck that!" he continued walking.

Lani walked up to Candy who was standing there with a smirk on her face. "Bitch you need to go, this is a family situation. Yo ass shouldn't have come in the first place."

"You're not mad at me honey, you're mad at her. My man is family and wherever he goes, I follow. Like Mykell said, she shouldn't have been running after some dick."

That's it. I snapped. Me, Lani, and Janae all pounced on the bitch at the same time. Ramone grabbed Janae because he knew better than to touch Lani, Micah grabbed Lani and Marco tried to get me but I had a death hold on that bitch's neck. Just when I was about to bang her head on the ground, my dad picked me up and pried my hands off of her.

"Daddy!" I scream and cried into his neck.

At that moment I felt like a little girl who needed her daddy to hold her and to tell her that everything was going to be okay.

Security came over and told us that we had to leave. So that's exactly what we did.

I walked out with my dad and looked over and seen Pop-Pop had Mykell hemmed up by his collar against his truck. He looked over and our eyes met. If looks could kill, I probably would have dropped dead on the spot.

Ramone

After a month, Lani still won't talk to me. Whenever I call her phone automatically goes to voicemail. When I go over to Pops house she always locks herself in the room and refuses to come out. This shit is getting out of hand. I understand that she is upset but she needs to realize that this shit happened before her.

I could've tripped and flipped out when I found out she was out to eat smiling in another nigga face with Ladybug and Janae. The other part that is killing me is not seeing my daughter. I'm getting closer to my son but can't even see my daughter.

I called Carmen and asked her to bring Keiyari over because I haven't seen him in a couple of days.

That shit that happened to baby Mell made me cherish the time I can spend with my kids.

I was sitting on the couch watching my son play with his toys when Lani walked through the door with Ranyla glued to her hip. *Oh shit.* I thought remembering Carmen was here also.

Lani was about to say something until she seen Carmen walking from the back.

"Oh, I hope I'm not interrupting family time." Lani said sarcastically.

"Lani come here," I said getting off the couch and walking towards her.

She backed up, "Nah, you stay right there. Me and Ny Ny will go; we didn't know you had company.

"Dada," Ranyla said smiling showing two teeth that wasn't there the last time I seen her.

"Le'Lani, give me my daughter and stop playing!" I was getting tired of her and these bullshit ass games she was playing.

"Fuck you Ramone!" she yelled before jumping in the car with Janae speeding off.

"Shit!" I yelled.

This shit is not supposed to be happening.

Kamil

I was sleeping good as hell when my I heard my phone ringing. I reached over and answered it without seeing who it was.

"Hello?" I said in a groggy voice.

"Are you sleep?" I heard the most beautiful voice say.

Neicey? I looked at the phone to make sure I wasn't dreaming.

"No, wassup?" I was fully awake now.

"I just need somebody to talk to, but if you're sleep I can call back another time."

"Nah, you don't have to do that. What's wrong?"

"Romell got hit by a car and he's in the hospital. His brain was swollen and he broke a couple of bones." Her voice was shaky and I could tell she was trying not to cry.

"Damn, I'm so sorry Neicey."

"Me too, Mykell blames me and he called me all type of hoe's and sluts. I think he's just mad because I don't want to be with him."

"It's not your fault Neicey. You had no control over the situation."

"I know but I just feel like a bad mother. Mykell was right, if I wouldn't have been worried about somebody else he wouldn't have got hit."

"C'mon now Neicey. You are not a bad mother. I've been around you so I would know, you would give your life for Romell. Fuck Mykell!"

"Yea, you're right. Listen, I gotta go. I'll talk to you later," she said before hanging up.

Talking to her put a smile on my face. To say that I was happy would be an understatement.

Chapter 10

Pop-Pop

Now I don't say much. I just sit back and observe but when things start getting out of hand, I don't think twice about saying what I feel. My damn kids are stressing me the fuck out. Mykell and Ramone carrying on like they don't give a fuck about their families, Neicey and Lani hanging with some other niggas because they're feeling neglected and want some attention. I'm 47 years old and I have no problem beating my kid's asses, I don't care how old they are or how grown they get.

Shit has gone too far and my damn family is threatening to fall apart. I'll be damned if I let that happen. It's time that I call a family meeting and get some shit in order, time to put my foot down and say enough is enough.

I got Le'Lani's ass living back with me, not to mention my granddaughter. Don't get me wrong, I love my kids, but I can't get my grown man on with a 1 year old and my damn 25 year old daughter moping around all that time.

I called all my kids telling them they better have their asses at my house by 7:00 tonight and I'm not taking any excuses.

* * *

I was in the den with Big Mone discussing the things I wanted to talk about tonight. At 6:30, my kids started pouring in the house. Of course Lani was already here but Micah and Janae were the first ones to get here. I took Ranee and gave her a kiss. I loved that little girl like I loved all my grandkids. I told Janae to take her to the play room I had built in for my grandkids.

Ramone, Mykell and Neicey all finally showed up, on time. I directed everyone downstairs to the TV room.

"As you all know, I called a family meeting because it's some shit going on that I do not approve of. It's time I put my foot down and say cut the bullshit." I turned to Ramone. "Now Mone, I told you to tell Lani about Keiyari the moment Carmen called you but you didn't listen and now look where it got you. You and your fiancé are living in two separate houses and you barely get to see your daughter."

I then went to Lani. "Baby girl, I understand that you are upset but what you need to realize is this situation happened before you two even got together. Yes, he should have told you about it from jump but he didn't. Keeping Ranyla from him is wrong. In the long run she will start to resent you for keeping her from her dad. Just because you two are in different about a situation doesn't mean that she should suffer."

"But daddy—"

"No buts Le'Lani. He has the right to see his daughter just like he has the right to have a relationship with his son. You're acting like he cheated on you and had a baby on you. Keiyari is three, Nyla is one. You two have only been together a little over two years. Do the math. Most women would be happy to have a man that wants to be in his kid's life."

"Now Mykell, I don't know how many times I'm going to have to talk to you about this shit. I told you a long time ago that you were going to push Neicey into the arms of another man. You didn't take heed to my warning and look what happened. She got into another relationship that almost cost her her life. This girl loves you without a doubt in my mind, she proved that when she took them damn bullets for yo ass. Me personally, I wouldn't have done the shit. You don't deserve it. You get mad because she doesn't want to be with yo dog ass and when you two should have each other's backs the most, you dog her out. How the hell does that sound? It wasn't her fault that Romell got hit by that car. You had a good woman on yo side but you fucked that up and you don't have anybody to blame but yourself."

I looked at Neicey. "Baby girl, I understand that you love that damn knucklehead over there and I also understand that you are tired. He will never find another woman like you, you took in his son, dealt with the other bitches, never complained or nothing, was always there when he needed you and all he did was give you his ass to kiss."

Mykell interrupted me. "Man, Pops—"

"Are you interrupting me Mykell? I just know like hell you not."

"Nah, go ahead."

"I thought so," I went back to Neicey. "Like I was saying, you're a good woman, but you need to open up your mouth and tell that nigga how you feel. If you don't like the shit he doing, call him out on it. Put him in his place, like you have done before. I know you feel like you're wasting your time but do it anyways. Mykell loves you just as much as you love him but he doesn't know how to show you. He has too much pride. But trust me baby girl when I say that he loves you, no doubt. He's never had someone to love him as hard as you since his mother. Now you just take care of my grandsons and stop worrying about his ass until he can you show you that he's ready to be with you."

"Micah and Janae, y'all are straight for now. Just don't make me have to sit down and talk to you too. Yall stressing me out now."

"Nah, we good Pops." Micah laughed.

"Good, now I'm going to watch my shows. Let y'all selves out. This meeting is adjourned," I said before heading upstairs shaking my head at my kids that I wouoldn't change for nothing.

Mykell

I can't believe my dad tried to make me out to be the bad guy. No lie though, he said some real shit. Leave it up to my pops to get everybody in order. I was playing Grand Theft Auto 5 with MJ when I heard the doorbell ring. *Who the fuck could this be?* I knew it wasn't Candy's ass because I gave that ditzy bitch the boot after I found out her and Neicey got into a fight at the hospital. I don't care if me and Neicey not on good terms, I'll never allow a bitch or nigga to disrespect her. That's kind of crazy seeing how I called her everything in the book at the hospital but I didn't mean it. I was just speaking on pure emotions. I really do regret that shit.

I got up to answer the door but nobody was there. A manila folder was on the ground with my name in black marker written across the front.

I sat on the couch and opened up the folder. "The fuck!" I said taking pictures out the folder.

"What's wrong dad?" MJ asked.

"Nothing MJ," I said never looking up.

I sat there looking at the pictures of Neicey and my son at the store, at her pops' house, my pops' house and everywhere. Then there were pictures of the scene when Romell got hit by the car. The last two pictures had me fuming. One was of Neicey getting out the shower reaching for a towel and the other was of Romell laying in his hospital bed.

I immediately jumped up and called Micah.

"Wassup Kell?" he ask out of breath.

"Mack, I need you to climb out the pussy real fast. Shit just got real, meet me at Pops' house in 10 minutes." I hung up without waiting for an answer knowing he would be there.

Next person I called was Ramone. "Mone, I need you to meet me at Pops' house in 10, oh and call Big Mone and tell him he's needed too."

"On my way now."

"One." I hung up.

"MJ, time to go. We gotta stop by yo Pop-Pop house real quick."

"Alright."

15 minutes later I was pulling up to my pops' house. I grabbed the folder with the pictures and hopped out the car with MJ right behind me. I walked in the house to see Big Mone, Little Mone, Mack, and Pops waiting for me.

"MJ go upstairs and keep an eye on Ranee." Micah said.

"Okay Uncle Mack."

"Alright Kell, we all here so what's up?" Pops asked.

"Somebody rung my doorbell today and when I went to answer, nobody was there but this folder was," I said giving him the folder.

He opened it and looked at the pictures before handing them to Big Mone. It was dead ass silent as the pictures went in rotation.

My pops opened the folder back up and took a piece of paper out that I must have missed earlier.

"You thought she was safe now? Well think again, I guess you're not as smart as you thought. You took one of mine, so I took one of yours. Maybe next time you won't mess with a bitch that was never meant to be yours." Pop read the note.

"These have to be some very bold muthafuckas to come to my house and violate my daughter. How the fuck did they even get in Baby Mell's room?" Big Mone asked.

"Good question Pops. How they hell did they do that shit and go unnoticed. The other question is who could this be?"

"Y'all don't think this could be Kamil do y'all?" Micah asked.

"Honestly, I don't put shit past nobody. I didn't think Kya had the balls to hire somebody to kill Neicey but she did."

Everybody looked up when they heard the front door open. In walked Neicey, Lani, Ranyla and Janae. They all had shopping bags in their hands, even Ranyla. We all just sat there staring at them.

"What? Who died?" Janae asked.

"Right, why y'all looking like that?" Lani asked.

"Nothing's wrong," Ramone said rubbing his head.

"Why you lying Ramone?" Neicey asked looking at all of us.

"I'm not lying."

"Well alright. Mykell, can I talk to you for a minute?"

I got up to see what she wanted. She walked up the stairs to my old room and put her bags down. I sat on the bed just staring at her, admiring her beauty. She's gotten a little thick in all the right places.

"The doctors said they are discharging Fat Fat from the hospital tomorrow. I'm going to be there because I don't want him to freak out if he doesn't see one of us," she said.

"What time?" I asked.

"At 12:00."

"Alright," I got up and walked up behind her and hugged her. I felt her tense up. I just kissed her neck and walked out the door.

We got some serious talking to do.

Reneice

I'm so happy I get to take my baby back home! The swelling in his brain went down, he only has one cast that goes all the way up his arm. Other than that, everything is good. The doctors said that he heals very quickly and he's a fighter. *Just like his mama*, I thought.

"Look mommy, I got a boo-boo." He pointed to the red cast on his arm.

"I see, mommy's big boy. Do it hurt?"

"No," he shook his head.

"Is that daddy's big man?" Mykell asked walking into the room.

"Daddy!"

"Hey big man. How you feel?"

"I feel good daddy."

"Good," Mykell said kissing his forehead.

"Mommy, you no say hi to daddy." Romell pouted.

"Hi Mykell," I said dryly, mad that Romell had to bust me out.

"Hi Neicey, we need to talk."

"Can it wait?" I asked.

I'm not trynna hear shit you talking about. If only you knew what I got up my sleeve, I thought.

"Yea that's cool."

*   *   *

Romell has been home from the hospital about two weeks now. I'm just waiting to make my exit. There are some decisions that I have to make for me and my son. I called Lakey the day Romell came home and told him to get ready for us. Romell and I will be moving to

Florida to start over. The only ones I've told are my daddy and Pop-Pop. *I hate to take Romell from his family but this is something I have to do.*

My thoughts were interrupted by the sound of my dad's voice.

"You all ready Ladybug?"

I sighed. "Yea daddy, I'm ready."

"What time does your flight leave?"

"Not till 1:00 in the morning."

"Alright, I'm going to take Romell with me, we're meeting up with your Pop-Pop and MJ so we can kick it before you leave."

"That's fine."

He walked over and kissed my forehead. "I'm proud of you Ladybug."

"Thanks daddy."

He walked out the room and I went to the bathroom. When I came out, Mykell was sitting on my bed.

"You scared the shit out of me," I said grabbing my chest.

"Neicey we need to talk."

"What do you want from me Mykell? You've already said what you had to say and made me feel like shit. You wanted me gone, so I left."

"I want you Neicey," he said in a low tone.

"What?" I asked confused.

"I said I want you," he said speaking louder this time. "I want you and my son to come home so we can be a family. Make it like it was before all the bullshit happened. You know, make it like it was when we first got together."

Before I knew it, I reached back and slapped the shit out of him. "I hate you Mykell! You never wanted me from jump. You were too busy fucking Kya and any other bitch. I loved you, I gave you my virginity. I was raped because of you, I lost my baby because of you, I was beat, my house was shot up, and I killed people. All for a nigga who never gave a fuck about me!" I yelled while punching him in his chest.

He just stood there and took it. That was it, I had finally reached my breaking point. He finally grabbed my hands and I broke down crying in his chest. "Shhh. I'm sorry baby. I'm sorry."

He gently kissed my tears away. As much as I hate this man, I love him at the same time. He tried to kiss my lips but I turned my head stubbornly. He took that as an opportunity to kiss my neck. I felt his hands travel down to the front of my pants. "No Kell." I tried to stop him but he only moved my hands out the way. He unbuttoned my pants and laid me on the bed, pulling my pants off.

He stared at me in my eyes while he took my thong off. He pulled me to the edge of the bed and got down on his knees. I tried to get up but he had a tight grip around my legs. I was mad at myself when I heard a gasp escape my mouth when his tongue found my spot.

My hand immediately went to the back of his head and I opened my legs wider for him. It was feeling too good, especially since I haven't had any sexual contact since weeks before I was in the hospital. No lie, Mykell is a beast in the bedroom.

"Ahhh!" I screamed out when I felt myself explode in his mouth. I was shaking like I was having a damn seizure. Mykell stood up and took his shirt off, there was that big ass tattoo of my name he got for my 21st birthday.

This nigga think he the shit. I thought as he got undressed. He climbed in the bed and put one of my legs on his shoulder while he penetrated me. I let out another moan against my will. He started pumping and kissing my neck. I felt something wet and looked up to see Mykell was crying. "I'm sorry Neicey. I love you."

"I love you too," I said even though I hate to admit it.

I pushed him off me. "Get on your back."

He did as I told him and I straddled him. I looked deep into his eyes while I rode him like my life depended on it.

I wiped his tears away and kissed his lips. *No matter how much I love him, I gotta make this move and do what's best for me.*

*   *   *

Mykell and I went at it all night. I laid in the bed thinking as Mykell slept. The clock read 11:45 and I knew it was time to make my move. I quietly crept out the bed and kissed Mykell softly on the lips before leaving out the room. I walked down the hall to the room Romell was sleeping in and seen my dad was getting him dressed.

"Daddy, Kell is in the room sleep. If he wakes up and asks for me, tell him you don't know where I went. Please?"

"I got you Ladybug, out just get out of here and get on that plane."

"Love you, daddy." I kissed his cheek.

"Call me when you get there."

"I will," I said as I picked up Romell and headed for the door."

The flight to Miami wasn't so bad. Romell slept the whole way there. When we landed, Lakey was there waiting for us.

"How was your flight Snook?" he asked taking Romell.

"It was alright."

"I'm happy y'all are here."

"I'm happy to be here," I said honestly.

"Like I already told you, I got a condo already set for y'all. It's got everything you need in there, including clothes. Which is why I told you not to pack anything. It's a car there waiting for you so you don't have to worry about transportation. Oh, and if you need me, I'm right around the corner."

"Thank you Lashaun, I really appreciate it."

"No need to thank me."

I looked at the beautiful scenery right before my eyes and was happy about moving down here. This is exactly what we needed. Mykell blew up my phone the whole flight, I feel bad about sleeping with him then just leaving him in the middle of the night but that's just how it played out.

Chapter 11

Lani

Since the family meeting, Ramone and I have been on better terms. We've been working on our relationship, I moved back in and I've gotten to know Keiyari better. Ever since he and Ranyla have met, they've been inseparable. He's so overprotective of his sister. I've even been getting along with Carmen. She made it very clear that she doesn't want Ramone, she just wants him to be a father to his son and I made it clear that I never had a problem with her.

I woke up to the smell of food being cooked. I went to the bathroom to brush my teeth and wash my face. When I got downstairs Ranyla was in her highchair and Keiyari was feeding her pancakes. Ramone was standing over the stove fixing some eggs.

"Hi Lani!" Keiyari said.

"Hey honey." I kissed him and Ranyla on the cheek and sat down at the table with them.

"Damn, I don't get no love?" Ramone asked faking jealous.

"Oooh! Daddy say bad word," Ranyla squealed.

"Watch ya mouth big head," I said before kissing his lips.

"Umm I missed that."

"Just nasty," Keiyari said shaking his head.

I laughed at him. "Mone have you heard from Neicey?"

Her ass been missing in action for three weeks. Nobody has talked to her or nothing.

"Nope but I got a feeling that Pops and my dad know where she at. She not just gon disappear without letting one of them know what was up."

"I agree, she could have at least let us know she was going somewhere though. I'm hurt, especially since we tell each other everything. Well, I thought we did."

"Baby don't feel like that. You know Ladybug doesn't make moves unless she has a good reason to, she won't be MIA for long. She'll call."

Yea so you say. Shit not the same without my best friend here with me.

Reneice

I've been in Miami three weeks now and I love it! I swear moving here was the best thing ever. I've truly been happy since I moved here. Lakey has been here with me all morning because for some reason for the past three days, I haven't been feeling too well.

I barely made it to the toilet before everything I ate that morning came up.

"Snook you okay?" Lakey asked wetting a rag and wiping my mouth.

"Yea, I think I caught a bug or something."

He just looked at me funny. "When was the last time you had a period?"

"Lashaun, you know the day after I started my period you, Mone, Howey, CJ and Jason took me to get on he shot and I haven't had one since." I shook my head at the memory of me sitting in the doctor's office with five grown ass men that were filling in the role of my daddy.

He chuckled. "I remember that day, you was mad at us for going with you. Talking about we were embarrassing you."

"I hated that."

"Okay then, let me ask you this. When was the last time you had sex?"

I got up from the floor and rinsed my mouth. Walking back into my bedroom I fussed at him. "I haven't had sex in…"

I stopped dead in my tracks as flashbacks of the night I left Detroit came back to my memory. Not one time did Mykell pull out.

"Oh my god, noooo!" I whined as I fell back on the bed. "That hazel eyed bastard has struck again."

"See, you stay here. Imma run and get you a test so we can know for sure," he said walking out the room.

Lord, please don't let this be happening to me again.

Twenty minutes later Lakey came back with some ginger-ale and a First Response Early Pregnancy Test. I took the test and went to the bathroom. I went and peed on the stick and put it on the sink and walked out.

"So wassup?" Lakey asked laying on my bed with his shoes on, knowing damn well I hate that shit.

I walked over to him and took his shoes off. "I have to wait three minutes."

"Cool, I got you some crackers and something to drink. I already put Fat Fat down for a nap so he'll be straight for about five hours." He laughed.

"Leave my baby alone," I said hitting him in his chest.

We sat and reminisced about the past before he reminded me about the pregnancy test.

"Can you look for me? Pleaseeee?" I pouted.

"Alright man." He got up and went to the bathroom.

"Ummm I think the two pink lines mean positive."

At that moment, I felt my heart fall into my stomach. *This can't be happening.*

Finding out I was pregnant yet again was the worst thing ever. Normal people under normal circumstances would be happy but I was the farthest thing from it. Having another baby, especially his baby was not in my plans. I know what I gotta do, it's the best choice for me right now.

I called Lakey up and told him my plans. He had my back, like always. I walked into my appointment with a heavy heart.

Do I really wanna do this?

I walked out of the clinic with my eyes full of tears. That was the hardest decision I've ever had to make in my life but I was satisfied with it.

Chapter 12

Kamil

A nigga could get used to this Miami weather. Don't get me wrong, I love Cali but this tropical weather is the shit. I can't even believe I'm here. I'm happy as hell but shocked at the same time. I'm staying at the Marriot on Bayshore Drive and as I was getting dressed to go see Neicey, I thought back to the phone call I received a few days ago.

I had just got out the shower when I heard my phone ring. I saw Neicey's name on the caller I.D. and I rushed to answer it. "Hello?"

"Hey Kamil, how are you?"

"I'm good ma, so what do I owe the pleasure of this phone call?"

"I need someone to talk to, besides I need to pick yo brain about something."

"Ok, that's cool. I'm listening."

"I actually want to talk in person."

"Uhh, you want me to come to Detroit."

She chuckled. "Oh I forgot you don't know, I moved to Miami two months ago."

"Oh shit, ok. I can do that."

"How soon can you get here?"

"How soon you need me?"

"Whenever."

"Alright, I'll look online and see what flight I can take then I'll call you and let you know."

"That's fine."

Now here I am three days later, in Miami. I drove to Terrazas River Park in anticipation of seeing Neicey. I knocked on her door and felt nervous as hell. Usually niggas would feel like this was a setup but I don't get that feeling.

The door open and I saw the most beautiful face that I thought I would never see again. *Damn she is so beautiful.*

"Hey Kamil," she greeted smiling.

"Wassup," I said leaning in for a hug.

My dick stood at attention when she hugged me. She still has that effect on me.

"Come in." she moved out the way so I could enter.

I nodded my head in approval, this was a bad ass condo and of course she got it decked out.

"Where's Romell?" I asked.

"He's with his Godfather."

"How's he doing?"

"Good, he's just ready to get his cast off now so he can move more but the doctor said he wants to wait two more weeks."

"That's wassup." I sat on her couch. "So what did you want to talk to me bout?"

She sat by me and sighed. "Ok, before I moved here I had this feeling that I was being watched or followed. You're the only person that I'm telling this because I didn't want anyone thinking it was you. I thought I had eliminated all the key players except for you. I could be wrong or I could just be paranoid. So I need to know who else was in on the plan to take me out."

Before I could answer, the front door came open. Romell came in running full speed.

"Mommy, look…" he stopped dead in his tracks when he seen me. "Mil?"

He never could say Kamil when he was little so he called me Mil.

"Wassup lil man?"

"Neicey, yo son is too much work." In walked one of this niggas I remember from Romell's first birthday.

"What the fuck is he doing here?" he said going behind his back for what I assumed to be a gun.

Neicey jumped up and I smirked. *I wish this bitch nigga would, he must have forgot I kill people for a living.*

Lakey

I walk in Neicey's house using the key she gave me and see this bitch nigga sitting there looking a little too comfortable for me. By instinct my hand went to my gun.

"Lashaun, chill. Not in front of Fat Fat," Neicey said.

I looked at Romell and thought he was the only thing saving this nigga life right now.

"Romell, go to yo room while I talk to yo mom."

"Bye, Mil," he said before taking off.

"Yo what the fuck is really good Reneice?"

"I invited Kamil here because I needed to talk to him about something that has been bothering me. Now you know me, you know I don't do shit without reason so chill. You can stay, listen and help out or you can leave and let me do this shit on my own like I intended to do. You pick."

I just looked at her stubborn ass then back to the bitch in the room. "I just want to know why?" I asked.

"If you would shut up and sit down, we could figure that out," Neicey sassed.

I just sat down and stayed silent to hear what he had to say.

"Ok, Kamil. You can continue," Neicey said sitting back down.

"Well, I was only in the D for about two months when Kya had approached me about some business. She said she was working with this girl to take somebody out. I never asked questions. Why, because I really didn't care, all I knew was I was about to get paid. They day I met you at Hooters, I didn't know you were my target. We got close, you moved in, we dated, I fell in love and I proposed. All that shit wasn't a part of the plan but it happened."

"So you knew I was going to get raped that night? You left early because you had some business to handle."

"I knew Kya wanted to have you roughed up, the rape was never supposed to happen. I left early to go talk to her about leaving you alone, when I got the call about you being in the hospital it killed me."

"So you knew about all the shit that was about to happen to her but not one time did you put her up on game or put two in each of them bitches' domes?" I spoke up tired of his bullshit.

"I know I should have told her, I wanted to tell her but I just didn't know how. I never even met the other bitch, she was the mastermind behind all of that shit. Kya's ass was too dumb to do shit."

"So who else was working with y'all?" I inquired.

"Them, but all I know is some other two niggas. She said one of them was her baby daddy but she never introduced us. She said she wanted to keep him on the low because she knew Mykell would surely kill his ass if he found out."

"You didn't at least get a name?"

"Naw," he said dryly.

This shit is too crazy.

Chapter 13

Mykell

It's been three months since Neicey decided to pull a damn disappearing act in the middle of the night. No lie, a nigga was hurt. I went over to her pops' house with hopes that we could work things out and put all the bullshit aside. I wanted to be a family, just the four of us. I guess I was the only one that felt that way. I thought I heard her say she loves me, no, I *know* I heard her say she loves me, but her ass pulled a damn hit it and quit it on my ass.

I knew the exact person to talk to about this shit, even though I knew I was going to get my ass chewed out.

"Hey Pops."

"Mykell," he said dryly.

"Why you gotta say it like that?"

"Because I already know what you want and all I have to say is I told you so."

"I know Pops," I sighed. "I know."

"I don't want to see you sit up here and cry like a lil bitch, I want to know what you are going to do about this situation," he said.

"I don't know Pops, I cried to her like a lil bitch and she played my ass to the left. I showed her how much I really loved her and her actions showed she don't really give a fuck."

"Oh, so you're telling me that you finally know how she felt. She finally treated you the way you treated her."

I took a deep breath and sat back. "Yea but I'm to the point where I say fuck it. I really give up. If she wanted to be a family then she never would have run off with my son. That was a bogus ass move."

"So basically what you're telling me is that fighting for your family really don't mean shit to you?"

"Not if I'm fighting a losing battle."

"If you really wanted her back and wanted to be a family again, you would do anything to get her back. Oh, and stop thinking that dick of yours can always fix something. That's the reason you're in this shit now," my pops said before getting up and walking out the room.

*   *   *

I've been trying to figure out who could have been trying to get at Neicey; another reason I hate that her ass disappeared. Her ass pulling some AWOL type shit and she still got somebody gunning for her head. I do know that whoever it is, is responsible for putting my son in the hospital. When I find out who it is, there will be hell to play.

"Dad, guess who I talked to today?" MJ said with a mischievous ass grin on his face.

"Who?"

"Mom," he said smiling.

I looked at him like he was crazy. "MJ don't play with me," I said seriously.

"Ok, you don't believe me." He laughed before running to his room.

Imma whoop his lil ass.

Janae

Here I am in the bathroom looking at a positive pregnancy test. I'm going through so many mixed emotions right now. *How will I tell Micah? Does he even want to have children? Am I ready for another child? Will he think I tried to trap him?*

"Yo baby, you don't hear me talking to you?" Micah said standing in front of me.

"Huh?" I said coming out of my thoughts.

"What's wrong..." he stopped when he noticed the stick in my hand.

"You're pregnant?" he asked.

I put my head down and let the tears fall from my eyes. "I'm sorry," I whispered.

"Sorry? Sorry for what?"

"I didn't do this on purpose and I wasn't trying to trap you."

He kneeled down in front of me. "I know, have you ever thought about the fact that I was trying to trap you?"

I looked at him like he was crazy. "What?"

"I knew what I was doing when I never pulled out, I wanted you to get pregnant. I think it's time we give Ranee a little brother or sister." He smiled.

"Are you sure?" I asked.

"Why wouldn't I be? You don't want any more kids?" he asked.

"I do, I just didn't know how you would feel about it."

He wiped my tears. "Girl stop crying. We gon be good, you, me, my lil mama and my junior," he said rubbing my stomach.

I laughed. "I can't believe you trapped me." I shook my head.

"Well believe it, now you're stuck with me for life."

I just smiled and kissed his juicy lips that I love so much.

"Girl, you better stop. That's how we ended up with this one."

God I love this man. I don't know what I would do without him.

Ramone

It feels so good to have my family back together. Me and Lani worked out our differences and have been fine ever since. I guess that family meeting helped us out. My kids love each other and are inseparable, their mothers get along fine so I don't have any baby mama drama. The only thing that is off in my life is my sister.

This is the longest we've ever went without communicating with each other. I still don't understand why she just up and left like that, my dad and Pops try to act like they don't know where she is, but I know better. I have a feeling that I know where she is and who she with, all I have to do is make a phone call for confirmation.

Micah

I can't believe I'm actually about to be a dad. I've always been around my nieces and nephews but to have one of my own is a feeling I can't even explain. I hope it's a boy so I can have me a little Micah junior running around. I already got my lil mama Ranee, even though I'm not her birth father, that girl is still my daughter. Now I'll have two kids to spoil.

Reneice

It has officially been seven months since I found out I was pregnant and here I am, big round belly and all. I know in the beginning I wanted an abortion but I changed my mind. An abortion really wasn't for me. I remember how I felt when I miscarried my first baby so why would I turn around and intentionally kill another baby?

I am nine months pregnant with a healthy baby girl. I can't wait to meet her. I feel real bad about the fact that Mykell will miss out on her birth; he hasn't missed the birth of any of his kids. Lakey and Kamil have been excellent at helping me with this pregnancy.

I can tell Kamil was upset when I told him I was pregnant again. He expected that if I got pregnant again, it would be with his baby. He fucked that up, not me. Even though he knew about all that shit that happened to me and even was in on it at one point, I forgave him.

I was sitting on the couch with my feet elevated because my feet were swollen as hell. Romell was being a good boy and rubbing his mommy's feet, Lakey was cooking dinner and Kamil was watching TV.

"Kamil, I never got a chance to tell you that I'm sorry for your loss." I smirked knowing damn well I didn't mean it.

"Who you talking about?" he asked confused.

"Kya."

He tilted his head to the side. "Kya?"

"Yea, you remember that day," I said thinking he was playing crazy.

"Neicey, Kya isn't dead."

"What!" I said scaring Romell. "I'm sorry baby."

"I thought you knew that," he said.

"How? I put a bullet in that bitch's head Kamil."

"Correction, that bullet grazed her head. She only had a flesh wound. When the ambulance came and got her, she was breathing."

'FUCKKKKK! Lakey!" I yelled.

"What the hell is wrong with you?" He asked with his face screwed up.

"We have a serious problem."

That was the biggest mistake I have ever made in my life. I should have made sure that bitch was dead, now this could come back to bite me in the ass.

Chapter 14

Mykell

I was fixing me and MJ breakfast when my phone rang. It said it was a Florida number. I wasn't going to answer but I decided against it.

"Hello?"

"Mykell, we have a problem," a man said.

"Who the fuck is this?"

"Lakey."

"Oh, my bad man. Wassup?"

"It's Neicey. She might be in trouble, hell I could be in trouble my damn self if she knew I was calling you."

Neicey? The hell he mean she in trouble?

"What you mean she in trouble? How you know where she at?"

"She been down here in Florida with me since she left, she begged me not to call and tell anybody. But enough of that, how soon can you get down here?"

"I'll book a flight right now."

* * *

I pulled up to the address Lakey gave me and I had to admit that I was fucking impressed. I called him and told him I was outside.

"I'm on my way down."

Five minutes later he walked out and came to my car.

He got in and sighed. "Okay look, there is somebody up there that I know you don't want to see but I need you to know that they are more useful to us alive than they are dead, especially now knowing this new piece of information I just found out. So when you get up there please try to keep it cool and don't react too fast."

"Who is it?"

"You'll see when you get in. second, Neicey cannot know you are here until it's time to reveal that. I don't want her crazy ass going off on me and putting a bullet in my ass."

I laughed. "Cool, man let's just do this."

We walked up to his condo. As soon as he opened his door I saw who was sitting on his couch and damn near pulled my gun on this bitch. I just stood there mugging this nigga and he had a smirk on his face.

"So we meet again," he said smugly.

I snapped. I punched that bitch right in his jaw. I kept punching him, letting all my frustrations out on his ass. He better be glad I left my fucking gin at home.

"Alright, enough Kell! Chill out man," Lakey yelled.

That bitch was wiping his mouth off looking like he wanted to kill me when his phone started ringing.

"Why you ain't tell me this nigga was here?" I snapped

"Yo! Lakey we need to go, the baby is on the way," Kamil said before Lakey could answer.

"Oh shit, come on y'all."

Twenty minutes later we pulled up at Mercy Hospital. I was confused as hell about what was going on but I went for the ride anyway.

Lakey ran ahead of us and went to the nurses' station. He ran into a room and I sat in the waiting room. Five minutes later he came out to come get me.

"Come on Kell."

I looked at this nigga like he was crazy. He laughed, "Nigga just come on."

I followed him to the room to see a very pregnant Neicey cussing the doctors out.

I looked at Lakey and he smiled. "Nigga will you get over there and help deliver yo baby?"

I didn't say anything, I just walked over to Neicey her eyes damn near popped out her head when she seen me.

"I hope you didn't think you was having his baby without me," I said grabbing her hand.

"Tell Lakey I'm going to kill him," she said breathing hard.

The monitor Neicey was hooked up to started to flat line.

"Diane! Go get the doctor and tell him we need to deliver this baby now! We're losing her," one of the nurses said.

I felt my heart drop in my fucking stomach when I heard that.

"Wait, what's wrong with my baby?" Neicey said panicking.

"Keep calm Ms. Peake, right now you just need to push and push hard," the nurse said.

I stayed quiet silently praying that my baby would make it. Hell, I didn't even know I was about to be a dad again until a few minutes ago.

"AHHHHHH!" Neicey screamed while pushing. My hand was going fucking numb from all that squeezing she was doing. The doctor ran into the room and took the nurse's place.

"Okay, one more big push," he said.

She pushed once more, then I heard the familiar sound that I could get used to. My baby crying.

""Hook her up to a machine and get her some oxygen now!" the doctor said.

She was born 6lbs 7oz and 21 inches long.

"Amyricale LeNae Jones," Neicey said looking at me. "Our little miracle baby. She escaped death twice."

I was wondering what she mean by twice but I'll leave that alone for now.

While Neicey was sleep, I went to go see my baby girl in the nursery. She is so beautiful, she looks just like Neicey but with my hazel eyes. That's a feature all my kids shared so I have no doubts about her being mine.

I asked the nurse if she could bring her back to Neicey's room and she said she would see if she was ready to come back. When I got back to the room, Kamil's bitch ass was in there and Neicey was woke.

"I hope I'm not interrupting anything," I said sarcastically.

"Actually, you are," Kamil said like he was annoyed.

"Frankly, I don't give a fuck. I already told you bitch, don't fuck with me. I already fucked yo lip up and you better be happy that's all I did."

"I got yo bitch," he said getting up.

"Hey guys, not today. Please?" Neicey begged.

At that moment, the nurse brought Amyricale in the room. I looked at her and all the bullshit left my mind.

"We make some pretty babies huh?" I asked.

"Yea, I guess you're good for something," she joked.

I could feel Kamil burning a hole in the side of my face. *Too bad bitch nigga, you'll never get to taste that again, ever.*

Reneice

Mykell hasn't left my side since I had Amyricale. I'm still confused as hell why he's even down here in the first place, but I know who called him. *Lakey*, his ass ain't slick. Today Amyricale and I get to go home. Romell loves his sister so much, he keeps calling her his baby. The moment I put her in her cute pink car seat, he tried to pick it up and carry her but she was too heavy.

"Man, let daddy handle that," Mykell said grabbing the car seat.

The drive back to my house was quiet besides Romell telling Amyricale all about his toys and how he wants to teach her how to play football. Out the corner of my eye I kept noticing Mykell stealing glances at me. When we got to the house Lakey and Kamil came out the house to greet us. I saw this look in Mykell's eyes when he saw Kamil. *I hope these two crazy niggas don't kill each other,* I thought as I walked in my house.

"Damn Kell, her ass look just like a mixture of you and Snook. She's a cutie though," Lakey said taking Amyricale out her car seat.

"Okay, y'all better be careful with my baby, I'm going to lay down. I'm still sore and a little tired," I said walking towards the stairs. "Oh, and no smoking around my baby."

I was getting undressed when I saw my bedroom door open and in walked Mykell. He just stood there staring at me like he had something on his mind. He was standing there looking sexy as hell, even though he only had on some baggy grey sweatpants, a black wife beater and some all black Air Forces, and he was wearing his black Detroit Tigers fitted cap low.

I climbed in bed with only my bra and panties on. I wasn't surprised when I felt him climb in bed with me. As much as I try to deny it, I can't. I truly love this man. No doubt about it. Now I was feeling bad that I just up and left him like I did.

He played with my hair like he used to do when we together. "Why you didn't tell me you were pregnant?" he finally asked.

I shrugged. "I wasn't going to keep her at first. When I was at my appointment for the abortion, I changed my mind. I wouldn't have been able to live with myself if I went through with it."

"Why you ain't tell me you was leaving? How you just gon leave a nigga like that?" he asked and I could hear the hurt in his voice.

"I'm sorry, I thought I was making the best decision for me and Fat Fat. Now I feel bad."

It was quiet for a minute. "Thank you," he said.

I turned around to face him. "For what?" I asked.

"For keeping my baby and giving me a beautiful daughter to spoil. Neicey, I love yo lil ass but I understand if you don't want to be with me. I can't say that I blame you. I know I was on some bullshit but I have thought about that shit and I don't want to lose you. If I have to deal with you being in my life only as a friend, then that's cool as long as I have you in my life," he said sincerely.

I just looked into his beautiful hazel eyes and saw the man that I fell in love with five years ago. I didn't know what to say so I just laid there in his arms until sleep consumed me.

*   *   *

I woke up to the sound of my baby crying. I jumped out of bed and threw a robe on. When I got downstairs, Romell was sitting on the couch with Amyricale is his arms and Mykell was coaching him on how to hold her.

I stood there and watched the three of them interact. The sight before me was beautiful. My baby girl was throwing a little fit so I decided to intervene.

"Maybe my lil mama is hungry," I said getting their attention.

"I changed Myricale diaper mama!" an excited Romell said.

"Did you baby?" I asked picking up Amyricale.

As soon as I picked her up, her crying ceased.

"That's mommy's girl," I cooed.

I walked over to her diaper bag and pulled out my breast pump. Since I was about to feed her, I might as well make her a bottle for later.

"Romell, come help me cook while ya mom feeds your sister," Mykell said.

"Alright, eat good, Pooh Bear," Romell said getting off the couch. "Mommy, her name Pooh Bear, okay?"

"Alright baby."

After I fed, burped, and rocked Amyricale to sleep, I went upstairs to take a shower. I was still a little sore but it wasn't anything I couldn't handle. When I got back downstairs, Mykell was just about done with the food. "Smells good in here," I said walking in the kitchen.

"Thanks mommy," Romell said.

"How you taking all the credit and all you did was put the garlic bread on the pan?" Mykell said.

I just shook my head and laughed at them. "What's on the menu fellas?" I asked sitting down.

"Spaghetti, fried tilapia and garlic bread," Mykell said.

"Sounds good."

I just sat back and watched Mykell and his mini-me work their way around my kitchen. I could not deny the fact that Mykell is a good father, no matter how horrible he was to me or anybody else.

Chapter 15

Lani

I was playing with Ranyla trying to get her to walk when my phone started to ring. I had a picture message from Mykell. *I wonder what this could be,* I thought as I clicked on the message. A picture of a beautiful baby girl with a head full of hair and hazel eyes popped up. The caption read *Amyricale LeNae Jones.*

"Ramone!" I yelled.

He came running down stairs. "What? What's wrong?" he asked out of breath.

I couldn't help but laugh because he had shaving cream all over his face. "I think you might want to see this," I said handing him he phone.

He looked at the picture for a few before speaking. "Yo, this baby look just like Ladybug when she was a baby."

I rolled my eyes. "Duh dumbass! That's her and Mykell's daughter."

"What? When? Where? How?" he said all in one breath.

"I don't know, give me the phone I'm about to call him."

I called his phone and he answered it on the third ring.

"Wassup knucklehead? You get my picture?" he asked and I could tell he was smiling.

"Yes I got it but me and Mone would like to know when the hell did this happen and why are we just now finding out about it?"

"Hell, I found out about her the day she was born, but I put it on her ass real good before she left and knocked her as up," he laughed.

I just shook my head at my brother. I heard fussing in the background.

"Hey mami!" Neicey said into the phone.

"Hey mami my ass! I'm so mad at you right now," I pouted.

"I know and I'm sorry. I'll bring her up there soon so you guys can see her."

"Hurry up chicken head, I can't wait to meet her. You know Mack knocked Janae's ass up, right?" I said telling it all.

"What? When?" she asked shocked.

"Four months ago."

"Oh my god, it's time for me to come home," Neicey whined.

"Yes hoe, I agree." I laughed.

"I will, I promise. I gotta go because my lil mama is getting cranky, she's ready to eat and her daddy is getting on her nerves. Give my niece and brother a kiss for me."

"Alright boo, will do."

I hung up the phone so happy. My girl actually sounded happy for once, hopefully her and Mykell can work their shit out and make it do what it do.

Micah

"C'mon Micah, I have to get up and get ready for my doctor's appointment," Janae whined as I slid between her legs for the second time that morning.

"If you would cooperate you could get up," I said as I pumped away while I threw one of her legs over my shoulder.

"But I...ohh...right there baby. That's my spot," she said as her eyes rolled in the back of her head.

"That's what I'm talking about, don't fight it. As a matter of fact, on yo knees."

She did as she was told. I pushed her back down while her ass was still tooted up. "Now what was all that shit you was talking? Huh?" I smacked her ass.

I heard my phone vibrating but I was too preoccupied at the moment.

"Baby...th...th...the phoneeeee!" she said while cumming at the same time.

I wasn't too far behind her. I shot a load right up in her.

"If you wasn't already pregnant, I bout would have knocked yo lil ass up with triplets just now," I laughed.

She hit me on my chest before climbing out of bed and heading to the bathroom. I picked up my phone to see Mykell had text me. I damn near jumped out the bed when I seen the picture of his baby. *Got damn, that nigga done struck again. Neicey ain't gon never be able to get rid of his ass now.* I shook my head at Neicey and Mykell, they just need to stop playing and be together.

Chapter 16

Mykell

I have been in Florida with Neicey and my kids for two weeks now and honestly, I didn't want to leave if they weren't coming with me. I don't know what got into Neicey last night but she had a nigga in his feelings last night. I was in my bed sleeping good in the guest bedroom when all of a sudden I feel her climb in bed with me and push her ass on my dick. She better be glad she gotta wait six weeks before she can get the dick or else I would've put it on her lil ass last night.

This morning I'm ready to just put it all on the table and see if I can get my family back. I walked in the kitchen to find Romell sitting at the table and Amyricale rocking in her swing while Neicey cooked breakfast.

"Damn girl, I might have to knock yo ass up more often if you keep getting thick," I said slapping her on the ass. Since having our daughter, her ass, thighs and breasts have gotten thicker and that shit look good as hell on her.

"Oooh daddy, you nasty," Romell laughed.

"I know," I laughed with him.

"Romell, hurry up so you can go clean that room like I asked you last night," Neicey fussed while putting a plate in front of me. She cooked bacon, cheese eggs, toast, pancakes, grits and hash browns.

"Damn girl, you know how to take care of yo nigga huh?" I joked.

"Last time I checked, I didn't have a nigga but I don't mind showing my *baby daddy* some love," she chuckled.

"Funny, smart ass."

"I'm done mommy. When I'm done cleaning my room can you go get me some ice cream?"

"I'll think about it Fat Fat."

"I want superman," he said before running out the kitchen.

"Yo Neicey, come here," I said scooting back from the table.

"What?" she said walking to me.

Pulled her down on my lap, "What was up with that shit you pulled last night?"

She shrugged. "I was in the mood to be held last night."

I looked into her eyes and realized that she wasn't the same eighteen year old girl that I fell for five years ago, she was now more mature and a woman. The shit she went through would break some women but not her, she came out stronger than ever and still smiles like she ain't went through shit.

"Look Neicey, I know I hurt you and I can say I'm sorry till I turn blue, but it won't change shit. I guess I did the shit because I always expected you to be there for a nigga. Even when you did leave me, I still thought I could have my way with you. That shit I said at the hospital, I didn't mean none of it. It wasn't your fault, everything that you went through was my fault only because I thought I could have my cake and eat it too, but that shit ain't me no more. I'm ready to settle down and make a woman my wife and give her my last name but I want that woman to be you," I said putting it all out there.

She sighed before speaking. "Mykell, you called me all types of hoes, sluts, made me feel like shit when I needed you the most, fucked that bitch Kya when I was suffering from depression and even before that, probably after. You brought a bitch up to the hospital with you when I was lying in a damn coma."

I tried to object but she stopped me. "Listen, I let you talk now let me talk. Even after all that I still loved you. Hell, even when I tried to hate you, I still loved you. As I'm speaking right now, I still love you. Now you're not perfect but neither am I. I don't want somebody that's perfect."

I wasn't expecting to hear her say that. "So what you saying? You want to be with me?" I asked hoping she would say yes.

"I'm saying, maybe we should start from the beginning, start fresh," she said smiling.

I didn't know what to say so I didn't say anything. I just kissed her soft lips and stuck my tongue in her mouth. We kissed for about five minutes until she finally broke the kiss.

"Alright, that's enough. I have to go pick up something for dinner tonight and I have to pick up your son some ice cream."

"Aight man, hurry back."

"I will," she said before heading towards the door.

To say that I was happy as hell would be an understatement. I finally got my family back and that's all I wanted.

*   *   *

It's been two hours since Neicey left and I had a funny feeling in my stomach. I just knew something wasn't right. She always answers her phone when I call, even when we weren't together.

I called for the twentieth time and finally got an answer.

"Baby, where you at?" I asked.

"Try again muthafucka! I told you it wouldn't be long before we got this bitch," an unknown voice said.

"Yo, who the fuck is this?" I yelled.

"I don't think you're in any position to be raising your voice Mykell," the caller taunted.

"If I don't have my girl back in the next hour, you a dead bitch," I said but they had already hung up.

I called the first person that came to my mind. "Pops, I need you like yesterday."

Reneice

I woke up in what looked like somebody's basement. It was cold and I didn't have anything on but my bra and panties. *What the fuck?* I was tied to a chair and couldn't move. The last thing I remember is I was walking to my car when I dropped my keys; I bent down to pick them up when I was hit in the head. The blow was hard but it wasn't enough to make me unconscious, so they put a rag over my face that I'm guessing was filled with chloroform.

The door opened and in walked the last person I expected to see. "Surprise bitch, I guess you thought I was dead huh?" Kya laughed.

I just looked at her and laughed. Ain't no way in hell I was about to let this bitch think she was putting fear in somebody, especially after I had beat her ass I don't know how many times.

"What's so funny? I don't think anybody told a joke," she said.

"Bitch, you're the joke. Who was the mastermind behind this one because I know yo simple ass ain't smart enough to think on yo own," I chuckled.

She reached back and slapped me in my face. Instantly I tasted blood. "Bitch you better kill me because if you don't, Imma kill yo ass, for real this time."

"Bitch please, I don't think you should be trying to make threats right now," she laughed.

I just looked at this bitch and thought of a way I could kill her ass slowly. She pranced her little ugly ass out the room.

"Let's see how much Mykell cares about yo ass after this, he doesn't give a shit about you, just like all the rest of us."

Lord please let me make it out of this one alive.

Lakey

My heart dropped in my damn chest when I got that phone call from Mykell. I'm so hurt, I don't know what to do. Amyricale must know her mom is not here because ever since I got her, she's been fussy. Pop-Pop just called and said they should be at the house in less than five minutes. He pulled his own private jet out for this one.

"Man, I finally got her ass to sleep. I'm about to put her in crib, I'll be back," Mtkell said looking stressed out.

As soon as he went upstairs, the doorbell rang. I opened it and in walked Ramone, Lani, Micah, his girl, Pop-Pop, MJ, and Big Mone.

"Wassup man?" I greeted Mone.

"Shit, ready for all this to be over with," he replied.

"MJ, Romell and Amyricale are upstairs. I just put your sister to sleep but I doubt she'll stay sleep, so I'm leaving you in charge of them while the grown folks talk," Mykell said walking downstairs.

"Alright dad."

The doorbell rung again, this time it was Kamil. As soon as he stepped in the room you could see the confused looks on everyone's faces.

Before I even knew what was happening, Ramone rushed Kamil and punched the shit out of him. "This shit is all your fault. You did this huh? This was your plan too? What the fuck you want?"

Big Mone was holding him back. "Look man, I know you are upset and all in yo feelings and shit but the next time you put yo fucking hands on me, I'll shoot you where you stand," Kamil threatened.

"Aye, y'all chill out. Mone, you not the only one hurting over this shit, we all are. Right now Kamil could actually be the person to help us find her," I said trying to be the voice of reason.

"Yea man, then after we get her back, we can both put a bullet in his dome at the same time," Mykell said.

I just shook my head. "Jason, Howie and Corey are on their way. But in the meantime, Kell did they say why they took her or if they were holding her for ransom?" I asked.

"No, whoever got her was using something to disguise their voice but all they said was, 'I told you this bitch was next.'"

"Kya," Kamil said pacing back and forth.

Everyone shook their heads. "Man, I regret not telling her that bitch was still alive. She just don't know when to leave shit alone," Mykell said.

"Kell, that's why I called you down here. Remember when I said Neicey was in trouble?"

"Yea."

"Well that's why. Kamil told Neicey that Kya was still alive. I guess he didn't know that she didn't know. Ever since then she been feeling paranoid. "

"That bitch just won't die," Micah said.

"I thought I was protecting her by not telling her. I never knew this shit would come back to bite me in the ass. That bitch got lucky twice, you would think she would have learned her lesson by now. I wonder who she working with this time?" Mykell asked.

"C'mon now Kell, you know that fuckin snake over there is related to that bitch. I know he got something to do with this. It's funny how he pop up in Florida then the next thing you know, her ass pops up too," Ramone said.

Everyone got quiet all of a sudden when Mykell's phone started to ring. We all looked at each other knowing that could only mean one thing.

Kya

I guess y'all thought a bitch was dead and gone huh? Well, think again. Bad bitches like me don't die. Maybe that bitch aim isn't as good as she thought. That's the second time she has shot me and I'm still breathing.

I walked down into the basement. Just the sight of this bitch had me ready to kill her ass but first I wanted to have a little fun.

"Wake up sleeping beauty," I said slapping her. "It's time for some fun," I said swinging my Louisville slugger. I swung it and hit her in her shoulder. She screamed out loud and I swear that shit made me horny.

"Oh cut it out. That didn't hurt you, not bad ass Neicey."

She looked up at me with fire in her ass. "I see that nose of yours is still crooked. You should get that fixed," she laughed.

I pulled her phone out my front pocket and dialed Mykell's number. "You can go ahead and say your last words because this will be the last time you ever talk to him again."

I put the phone on speaker. "Hello?" that sexy voice said.

"Hey Kell," she said.

"Baby, where you at? How are you? Did they hurt?" he asked making me sick.

"I'm alright. Kell I just want you to kiss my babies for me. Tell all three of them that I love them. I already know you're a good father and will raise them the best you can so I'm not worried about that. I just want you to know I love you."

"Neicey why you talking like that?" he asked.

Before she could answer, I brought that bat down on her knee.

"Ahhhhh!" she screamed.

"What the fuck? Neicey? Talk to me baby, please?"

I hung up the phone. I was tired of him acting like he really gave a damn about this bitch. Fuck him and fuck her.

I walked out and called my baby daddy's brother. I know he would love to get in on this plan.

Chapter 17

Ramone

It's been four fuckin days since my sister was taken and I feel like I'm losing my damn mind. I can't even begin to imagine what she is going through or what they are doing to her. I just know that fuck boy Kamil has something to do with this shit. His ass is supposed to be dead anyways. Every time he brings his ass around, some shit happens to my sister.

My boys came down here and we been racking our brains trying to figure this shit out.

"Wassup Kell, Mone. How ya'll holding up?" asked Lakey.

"Shit I'm barely holding on," I answered.

"Man, I gotta keep holding on for my kids," Mykell said.

"So they ain't called back or nothing?" Corey asked.

"Nope," I said.

"I told Kamil to try to get in touch with Kya to see if she had anything to do with this shit. Something in my gut is telling me this bitch is behind all of this," Lakey said.

"You think she working alone this time?" I asked.

"I doubt that, that bitch was never too bright. I wouldn't put shit past her ass though," Mykell said.

"Hold up y'all," I said reaching in my pocket for my phone. "Wassup baby?"

"Mone! Y'all need to get to Neicey's house and get here fast," Lani said worriedly.

"What's wrong?" I asked hearing the distress in her voice.

"Just get here please?"

"We on our way."

"Wassup man?" Mykell asked.

"That was your sister, she told us to get to the house A.S.A.P"

* * *

We got to Neicey's house in twenty minutes. When we walked in the house, everyone was looking down and out.

"Okay, we here. What's wrong?"

"We got some more pictures," Janae said handing me a folder.

I opened it and almost broke down. Neicey's face was swollen to the point where you couldn't recognize her and she was only wearing panties and a bra. One of the pictures showed her tied to a bed with a man with a mask on laying on top of her.

I couldn't take it anymore. I threw the pictures on the ground and punched the closest wall to me.

Lani came rushing over to me. "Baby, it's going to be okay," she said grabbing my hand and looking over it. "I'll get you some ice."

"Why the fuck do this keep happening to her! Ladybug ain't never did shit to nobody but she can't seem to catch a fucking break. Word, on my mother's grave I'm killin any and everybody who got something to do with this shit!" I yelled.

Mykell picked up the pictures and you could literally see the color drain from his face. Amyricale started crying and he went to pick her up. I swear this is the first time I've seen him cry. This shit was tearing all of us up.

Mykell

I just took my baby girl up to my room to get away from everybody. It seemed like she was the only thing keeping me sane right now. I feel like all this shit is my fault. If I never would have pursued Neicey, none of this would be happening to her. Because of me, her life is a living hell. I've never been the type of nigga to pray because I felt like God didn't wanna hear anything I had to say, but right now praying was the only thing I could do.

"God, I know I'm not the best man in the world and I've done my fair share of sinning but I just ask that you protect Neicey and bring her out of this alive. She doesn't deserve this, all she wants is to be happy but it looks like that will never happen. If you bring her home, I promise I will do right by her and actually make her my wife. Please God, just let her make it out alive and let us find her to bring her home where she belongs. Amen."

"Amen," I heard from behind me. I turned around to see my dad standing there.

"Why Pops? Why does this keep happening?"

"I don't know son. But I do know that you can't let this break you. That little girl in your arms and your sons need you. Don't worry, we'll find her and it will be soon," he said before kissing Amyricale and walking out of the room.

I looked in my daughter's eyes and she smiled at me. "I promise no matter what I'm bringing mommy home, baby girl. That's my word," I said, making a promise that I was sure to keep.

Reneice

I can't take it no more. I'm ready to give up. I'm tired physically, mentally and emotionally. My body can't take it anymore, the abuse and the raping, it's all starting to take a toll on me. I haven't eaten or had anything to drink since I've been here, my right eye is swollen shut, my body hurts like hell and I'm weak.

I don't understand why this shit keeps happening to me. Why does God keep punishing me? My life isn't supposed to be like this, I'm supposed to be a very successful lawyer, living in a nice home, with a husband, and some kids.

I heard the door open and I already knew what time it was. The same routine has been happening since I been here. I would get raped and that bitch would stand there with a smile on her face like she was enjoying this shit. I just laid there and took it. I refused to shed one tear. I was not going to let this bitch know that she was winning.

Mykell please hurry up and come get me.

Kamil

I just know that Kya is behind this shit. Sometimes I can't believe that the scandalous bitch is my cousin. I've been trying to call her for the longest but she won't answer the phone. She's knows I'm on to her ass. So I decided to play her game. I'll make her think I'm on her side and her gullible ass will fall for it.

I changed my number so she won't recognize it when I call. I paced my hotel room back and forth waiting for her to answer.

"Hello?" she answered and I damn near jumped for joy.

"Damn, a nigga gotta go through all this just to talk to his cousin?" I said sarcastically.

"What do you want Kamil? I'm kind of busy."

"Doing what?" I asked.

"Minding my business," she replied smartly.

"I know you up to something, so let me in on it," I said, hoping she would take the bait.

"What makes you think I'm up to something?"

"Because I've known your conniving ass all my life so I know where you're up to something."

"I'm all the way in Florida Kamil," she said confirming what I already knew.

"You act like a nigga can't travel," I said.

The line was quiet for a while. "Alright, Imma text you an address I want you to meet me at tonight. You better not be on any bullshit either Kamil."

"Never baby girl." *Dumb ass.* I thought as I smiled.

"Whatever," she said before hanging up.

Just like taking candy from a baby. I knew her dumb ass would fall for it.

Two minutes later she texted me the address and what time she wanted me there.

I sped all the way to Neicey's house. I knew her brother and Mykell wanted to kill my ass but fuck them. I wasn't doing this for them, I was doing it for Neicey. I love her just as much as they do.

I knocked on the door and waited for someone to answer.

"Hello Kamil," her dad said when he opened the door.

"Hello," I said walking in the house. "I came because I think I can have Neicey home by tonight," I said getting straight to the point.

"How so?" he asked.

"Well I finally got in touch with Kya, she said she had a job for me but she's all the way in Florida, which we already knew. She texted me an address she wants me to meet her at tonight."

"What time we gotta be there?" Mykell asked from behind me.

"She said midnight," I said.

"We'll be ready."

"We all can't go in at the same time. If she does have Neicey, she'll probably kill her if we just go in blazing. I have to go in first and make her think everything is cool."

"Then how the hell are we supposed to know when to come in?" Ramone asked.

"That's why I'm here, so we can come up with a solid plan," I answered.

"Well, let's do this shit then," Mykell said.

We sat down and worked out a solid plan that would get Neicey out safely and home.

*   *   *

It's show time, I thought as I got out of my car and walked to the house that looked abandoned. Kya opened the door and looked around like she didn't expect me to be by myself.

"The hell wrong with you?" I asked.

"Nothing, just come in," she said.

I followed her to the back of the house and down some stairs that led to the basement. We walked to a little room in the basement and that's when I saw her, my heart broke and it took everything in me not to put a bullet in Kya's fuckin head.

"It's just us?" I asked. Looking at Neicey.

"For now," she said.

"Is she dead?" I asked fearing the worst.

"I hope so. She might just be unconscious though. I must say that bitch is a trooper though, not one time did she cry or give in," she said like she was mad.

I heard footsteps upstairs. I already knew who it was, but I still drew my gun just to be sure.

"Hmm he's early," Kya said walking to the stairs.

Wrong idea. I thought.

Mykell

I waited ten minutes like I was supposed to. I was getting tired of all this waiting shit, I was ready to go in and kill everybody. I walked to the front door and shook my head because this bitch didn't have enough sense to lock the damn door. I followed the voices to the back of the house and sent Micah a quick text.

Micah: *I'm in.*

I walked to the stairs and heard Kya talking, she sounded like she was coming my way. *Perfect.* I thought reaching for my gun. I had a smirk on my face when I saw Kya walking up the stairs. She didn't notice me until my gun was right in her face. She looked like she was about to shit bricks.

"Take yo stupid ass back downstairs."

"Shit," she said as walked down the stairs backwards.

I followed her to a little room, Kamil was in there standing next to Neicey. I just knew she was gone by looking at her, she didn't even look like she was breathing.

"Tell me she ain't dead, man."

"Naw but her pulse is real faint, we have to hurry up and get her out of here," he said, reaching to pick her up.

"Don't touch her muthafucka," I heard from behind me, followed by the sound of a gun cocking. I looked at Kya and she had a smirk on her face. I turned around and found myself looking at a nigga I was cool with once upon a time. A nigga I actually looked at as a brother. *I should have known his ass was in on it too.*

"Don't look so happy to see me," Boogie said.

"Really nigga? This how we doing it now? What part of the game is this?" I asked with venom dripping from my voice.

"Fuck you nigga! What part of the game was killing my fucking brother? All over a bitch that wasn't even yours to begin with," he spat.

"Yo! Watch yo fucking mouth. If yo bitch ass brother wouldn't have been like yo grimy ass and out here raping women, I wouldn't have had to kill his ass."

"Mykell fuck him, we have to get Neicey to the hospital," Kamil said.

I turned to look at her, which was a wrong move on my part. I saw Boogie moving out the corner of my eye and I turned around to, shoot but it was too late. I was hit in my shoulder but I still got off a shot that hit him right in the middle of his eyes. I heard another shot and turned just in time to see Kya hit the floor. I looked at Kamil and he shrugged his shoulders. *This nigga just killed his fucking cousin,* I thought as I emptied my clipped into her body to make sure she was dead this time. Kamil picked up Neicey and carried her up the stairs and I followed. I looked back at Boogie, *unloyal ass nigga.*

Kamil put Neicey in the backseat of my car while I hopped in the passenger seat. "Me and Lakey will follow y'all," he said.

I looked over at my brother who was sitting in the driver's side. "Mack—" I said, but he cut me off.

"I already know nigga. Traffic laws don't even exist to a nigga right now," he said speeding away.

I looked in the backseat and looked at Neicey. I felt my blood boiling all over again. I'm just happy this shit is finally over with.

Reneice

I woke up to the sound of a monitor beeping. I looked around and noticed I was in the hospital. *How the hell did I get here?* I tried to sit up but I was too weak.

"I don't think that's a good idea," I heard my dad say. I looked at him and he looked like he hadn't had any sleep.

I was about to say something but two well-dressed men walked into the room. "Ms. Peake, I'm Officer Zaluchi and this is my partner Officer Calvin. We have a few questions to ask you, if you don't mind," the tall one with ocean blue eyes said.

"Is that really necessary right now?" myMy dad asked. "She just woke up."

"Yes, we would like to get it out the way," Officer Calvin said.

"Ms. Peake do you remember what happened?" Officer Zaluchi asked.

Not really in the mood for this I just shook my head no.

He looked at me like he didn't believe me. "Do you know who did this or who would have a motive to do this?" he asked.

I just shook my head again hoping he would get the hint and leave.

"Alright Ms. Peake, if you do seem to remember anything please give us a call," he said, trying to hand me a card but my dad took it instead.

"We'll call," he said.

The officers left, then it was just me and my dad. "You know I'm not calling them right?" he said, coming to adjust the bed so I was sitting up some.

I nodded my head, "I know."

In walked Mykell with his shirt off and a bandage on his shoulder. He walked over to me and tried to kiss me but I turned my head. He looked at me funny then went to sit down in a chair by my dad.

It's crazy because I was begging for him to come and save me but now that I'm looking at him, I feel like he's the enemy. I'm starting to feel like all this shit is his fault. No doubt I love him, but I feel like all the shit I have been through wasn't even worth it.

"Where are my kids?" I asked breaking the silence.

"At home sleep," he said.

I just looked at him. I was starting to wonder if I spoke too soon when I said I wanted to be in a relationship with him again.

A doctor walked in the room during our intense staring battle.

"Hello Ms. Peake, I'm Doctor Martin. How are you feeling?"

"Horrible." I kept it short.

"I bet, you have a dislocated shoulder, a few cracked ribs, your right eye is swollen so much that you can barely open it, you have a lot of bruises, and you were dehydrated and famished when you got here so I understand why you would feel that way."

Hearing all that, part of me wished I would have died in that room. I heard Mykell asking him some questions but I just zoned out.

Chapter 18

Ramone

I didn't want to leave my Ladybug down there in Florida but I trust and know she's in good hands down there with Mykell and Lakey. I called every other day to check on her. But now I have other issues that I need to take care, one of them being Le'Lani. Lately she's been acting real funny, she's either sleeping all day, snapping on me or Ranyla or she's gone all day. I got a feeling she's pregnant.

She's been gone for two hours so I decided to call her and see where she's at. Her phone rang four times before she answered. "Hello?" she answered.

"Yo where the fuck you at?" I yelled.

The line got quiet, I had to look at the phone to make sure she didn't hang up. "You not gon say shit?"

"I'll be there in a minute," she said before hanging up.

I just shook my head. Something was up with her ass and I was about to find out but that shit would have to wait because my son was on his way over. I went to Ranyla's room to check on her and she was knocked out. She reminded me so much of Ladybug and Amyricale. I bent down and kissed her forehead and headed out her room. By the time I reached the bottom of the stairs, somebody was knocking on the door.

I opened the door for Keiyari and Carmen. He ran up and started punching me in my legs and I picked him up and tossed him in the air, our little routine we did every time we saw each other.

"Where Ny Ny and Lani?" he asked.

"Why, you don't want to see me?" I asked tickling him.

Carmen laughed. "He made me rush all the way over here because he bought Ranyla and Lani something," she said handing me his bags.

"Is that right?" I asked.

"Yup," he giggled.

I looked up to see Lani pulling in the driveway on the side of Carmen's car. She got out with bags of food in her hand.

"Hey Carmen, he lil man," she said kissing Keiyari's cheek.

"Lani, I got something for you!" he said excitedly.

"Really? What you get me?" she asked smiling.

"It's a surprise."

"Oh I love surprises," she smiled before walking in the house.

"I'll be here to pick him up Sunday at 8:00," Carmen said before kissing Keiyari and leaving.

I went in the house in search of my fiancé, it was time for us to talk. I put Keiyari down on the couch and turned on cartoons for him. I found Lani in the kitchen putting food away and getting ready to start dinner.

I walked up behind her and put my hands on her hips that looked like they were spreading. "Yo wanna tell me where you been all day? I missed you."

She turned around to face me. "I went to the mall and did a little shopping then I went to the store for dinner," she said looking at me.

"Aight, I got something I want you to do for me though," I said kissing her neck.

"What?"

"Hold up, I'll be back," I said walking upstairs to our room. I went straight to our bathroom and got the pregnancy test I bought earlier.

I walked back into the kitchen. "Here," I said handing her the pregnancy test.

"Are you serious?" she asked taking it.

"Why wouldn't I be?" I asked looking at her.

"I can promise you that I'm not pregnant but if you want me to take it I will," she said, walking towards the downstairs bathroom.

I heard Ranyla whining so I went upstairs to get her. "Hey baby girl, I see you finally woke up."

She just looked at me and smiled. She had a mouth full of teeth and was saying little words here and there. "Guess who's here to see you?" I said walking into the living room.

She got so happy when she saw her brother. "Hey Ny Ny, look it's SpongeBob." Keiyari said.

"Pongebod," she said trying to talk. I just stood back and watched my kids. I loved the relationship that they have. It reminds me of how close Ladybug and I are. I went to the bathroom to check on Lani. I opened the door to her looking like she just seen a damn ghost.

"Well?" I asked dying from anticipation.

"It's positive," she said with tears in her eyes.

I just took her in my arms and held her tight. "It's going to be okay baby. Don't worry."

I rubbed her back as she sobbed in my chest.

Lani

I cannot believe this. This just can't be happening to me, not like this. I needed somebody to talk to. I hate that Neicey is all the way in Florida especially at a time like this.

I knocked on the door and waited for somebody to answer. I gasped when the door opened. The sight before me had me weak in the knees. The fine specimen was standing before me with nothing on but basketball shorts and I almost forgot why I was here.

"Wassup ma?" Zamier asked pulling me in for a hug.

I inhaled his scent and he smelled just like Guilty Gucci cologne.

"Thanks for letting me stop by." I smiled.

"No problem. You said it was important, so wassup."

I took a deep breath. "Umm I'm pregnant," I said just coming right out and saying it.

His facial expression went from shocked to concern in a matter of seconds.

"Is it mines?" he asked the question I've been dreading to hear since I found out.

Alright so I haven't been honest. Yes I have been sleeping with Zamier since me and Ramone broke up. In the beginning it was just a harmless friendship then one night things got a little heavy and one thing lead to another. What should have only happened one time ended up happening on several occasions. I would be lying if I said I didn't enjoy it. I know I should feel bad or some type of regrets but I don't. I have a man at home that I love, no doubt about it, but at the time I was hurt and wanted him to feel the same pain I felt.

Now I dragged a real good person and friend in the middle of my bullshit.

"Honestly, I don't know. I just took the test yesterday so I'm not sure how far along I am or if I even want to keep it."

I noticed him tense up at the last part. He looked at me with sad eyes. "Look Le'Lani, I know you and ya boy back together and want to work things out. I respect that, I really do but it's a chance that this baby might be mine which means I don't want you getting an abortion. I'm pretty sure yo boy would feel the same way. If we find out later on down the line that this baby is mine, I'll take it and raise it. I know this might cause some problems in yo relationship be you gotta think about how I feel," he said sincerely.

I just looked in his eyes and understood where he came from. I don't have anyone to blame for this but myself. Even though we haven't slept together since before I left for Florida I still feel like shit about this whole situation.

"Alright, I'm going to make a doctor's appointment to find out how far along I am and we'll go from there," I said getting up to leave.

"Thanks for understanding," he said hugging me.

Once in my car I released the breath I didn't even realize I was holding. One thing I know for certain is that no matter who the daddy is, this baby is a part of me and I wouldn't feel right getting rid of it. I made my bed so I gotta be woman enough to lay in it.

Chapter 19

Mykell

To say that a nigga is stressed out would be an understatement. Once again it was a damn strain on me and Neicey's relationship. It seems like all that shit we said before she got kidnapped was never was even said. She's been real distant lately, not just from me but from the kids also. Amyricale will try to reach for her and Neicey will walk right past her like she's not even there. I haven't seen her like this since she fell into that deep depression when she was raped and beaten the first time.

If it wasn't for Lakey and that nigga Kamil helping me with the kids, I don't know what I would do. Kamil and I decided to put our differences aside and be men. This wasn't the time to be going at each other's throats with Neicey being the way she was. The bruises and swelling were gone, she wasn't using crutches anymore and her shoulder was better but that was nothing because the emotional scars and pain was still there.

Lakey thought it would be a good idea to take the kids to Disney World since they haven't been yet since we've been in Florida. I tried to get Neicey to come with us so she could get some fresh air and have some fun, but she refused.

"This was a good idea man. I don't know why I didn't think of this," I said as we pulled up in Magic Kingdom.

"Look daddy!" Romell said excitedly.

I looked back and smiled at my kids back there looking like triplets. Amyricale was in her car seat making spit bubbles. I don't care if she was too young get on any of the rides, wherever I went, my princess went.

While MJ and Romell ran wild from ride to ride, Lakey and I followed close behind them with Amyricale in her stroller.

"So what's up man, how she doing?" Lakey asked.

I just shook my head. "Not good man. I'm just scared she's going to end up like the last time," I said being honest.

"I understand, shit. This shit she's been through would drive most muthafuckas crazy. She's a strong woman though, I'll give her that," Lakey said.

"I know, I just feel like if she never would have met me, none of this shit would have happened to her."

"Man chill on that. I've known Snook all my life and I can tell you right now that her lil ass is happy with you. Wherever somebody mentions your name she gets this sparkle in her eyes. She loves you and it's not hard to tell," Lakey said

"I feel like we just need to get away for a while. Just me and her, get to know each other again and remind each other why we fell for each other in the first place," I said bringing my thoughts to life.

"Then do that, go away to Jamaica or the Bahamas or something."

I just nodded my head in agreement. That didn't sound like too bad of a plan.

"Dad, I think Fat Fat is sick," MJ said running to me.

"I ran over to Romell and he looked like he was ready to throw up. Right when I was about to pick him up, he turned his head and let everything up.

"Alright lil man, looks like we're going to have to cut this trip short," I said carrying him back to the car. *It was fun while it lasted.*

Reneice

I feel real fucking worthless right now. I don't understand how much more God wants me to hurt and suffer. I'm only 24 years old and I've been raped not once but twice, beaten to the point where I was barely recognizable, not once but twice. My life was not supposed to be like this. It seems like I just can't catch a fucking break. On top of that. I'm pregnant with a baby that's a product of rape. I don't want people walking around feeling like they have to feel sorry for me. I just know this is not the plan God had for me. This is it, I don't want to live anymore.

I walked in the closet and pulled out a shoe box that held my nickel plated .45. I stood in front of the big mirror on my dresser and watched as the tears fell. I loaded a bullet into the chamber and cocked the gun before placing it to my head. *Lord, forgive me for what I'm about to do. I just can't take it anymore, watch over my kids and Mykell, and protect them,* I silently prayed. Just when I was about to pull the trigger, the door to the bedroom opened.

"What the fuck yo!" Mykell yelled. He rushed over to me and tried to take the gun from me but I wouldn't let it go.

"Let it go Reneice!" he yelled. We wrestled with it for a few before I finally gave up and ran to the bathroom. I slammed and locked the door before turning to the cabinets to find some pills I could take.

Bang Bang Bang! "Open the fucking door Neicey!" he yelled. I ignored him and grabbed the bottle of ibuprofen, I poured a handful into my hand. Before I could even put them to my mouth, the door came crashing down.

BOOM!

Mykell slapped the pills out my hand. "Ahhhh!" I screamed.

He grabbed me by my collar. "Really Reneice? That's how you gon do it? Shit is that serious that you trynna off yourself!" he yelled with tears in his eyes.

I just broke down and cried in his chest. "Just let me die Kell, please, just let me die," I cried.

He slid to the ground with me in his arms. He rocked me back and forth as we both cried. I had finally reached my breaking point.

"Y'all okay?" MJ asked walking into the bathroom looking confused.

I was crying so hard I couldn't even answer him.

"Yea man, just go watch yo brother and sister till I get down there," Mykell spoke with a shaky voice.

"I just want to be happy Mykell, is that too much to ask for?" I cried.

I cried so much that I eventually felt my eyes getting heavy. The last thing I remembered was Mykell carrying me to the bed and laying me down in his arms until I drifted off to sleep.

Lakey

When I got the phone call from Mykell telling me what Neicey tried to do, I almost broke down. I knew she was hurting but I didn't think it was that bad that she would try to commit suicide. That don't even sound like her to do something like that. I told Mykell that I would be by to pick up the kids so they could stay with me for a little while. He agreed because he didn't want them to see her like that and I don't blame him.

"Thanks again man, I really appreciate this," Mykell said as I grabbed the kid's bag.

"Man you don't have to thank me, that's what family is for. I'll keep them for as long as you need me to," I said picking up Amyricale's car seat.

"Alright, I'll call to check on them later. She's upstairs sleeping now so Imma let her get some rest before we talk about this shit."

"Alright, stay up man."

"I'll try," he said looking hurt. "MJ, Romell, y'all be good."

"Alright dad," they said.

I'll be sure to say a special prayer for my Snook tonight, I thought as I got the kids settled in my truck.

Chapter 20

Ramone

I was happy as hell when I found out that Lani was pregnant again. At first she wasn't but she finally warmed up to the idea.

Lani was downstairs cooking breakfast while I was in the shower. When I got out, I heard her phone ringing. I went to see who it was when I noticed she had a missed call and a text message from a Zamier. *Who the fuck is that?* I thought as I clicked on the message.

Zamier: Wassup ma? I tried calling you but I figured you were busy. Call me or stop by so we can talk about the baby situation and so we can figure out what we gon do.

I was seeing fucking red. What the fuck this nigga mean they need to talk about the baby situation? I just know her ass wasn't fucking another nigga. I hurried up and threw on some jogging pants and rushed downstairs. I rushed up on her and grabbed her by the t-shirt she was wearing.

"Who the fuck is Zamier?" I asked through gritted teeth.

She just looked at me and rolled her eyes. "A friend," she said like she had an attitude.

"Really now? Then what the fuck his ass want you to come see him about the baby then? I just know like hell you ain't fuck this nigga," I said, getting so close to her face that I was damn near nose to nose with her ass.

"He might be the father," she mumbled.

It took everything in me not to put my fucking hands on her. She better thank God that she's pregnant and I respect females.

"Get yo shit and get the fuck out my house and don't think for a second you taking my damn daughter. Or is she even mine?" I asked with venom dripping from my voice.

She just laughed and shook her head like I told a joke or something. "Alright. I'll leave but you got me fucked up, bent wrong and twisted if you think for one second that I'm leaving without *my* daughter nigga," she said storming out the kitchen.

*   *   *

Hearing Lani say that's it's a possibility she could be carrying another nigga's child had me fucked up but what had me even more fucked up was the fact that she was acting so damn nonchalant about it.

I went to the one person I knew I could talk to about anything. My senior.

"Wassup dad?" I asked as I walked through his door.

"You tell me. You look like you're about to kill somebody," he said sitting across from me on the couch.

"Man, Lani told me that she's carrying another nigga child. Well, it *could* be his," I said.

He just looked at me shocked. "Damn," he said shaking his head. "So she cheated on you and got pregnant?" he asked me.

"Yea...no. I mean, I really don't know. I didn't ask any questions, I just told her to get her shit and get out."

"And your daughter?" he asked.

"She's with her," I said.

"Wow, so you have your woman and daughter out there on the streets and you didn't even try to talk to her about the situation. That was smart," he said sarcastically. "You must have forgot that little period when you two broke up," he said reminding me of that little spell me and Lani went through.

"What the hell was I supposed to do? She fucked somebody else, I didn't. She acted like she didn't care so why should I?"

"Did you see any signs of her cheating? Did she ever come in smelling like another nigga? Did her pussy feel any different? Did she stop fucking you? Was she acting funny?" he asked all in one breath.

I thought about it and the answers to all those questions is no.

"Oh shit," I said realizing that I fucked up and made the situation worst.

"Yea, you messed up. Now get out my house and go get your daughter and girl," he said.

What the fuck am I gon do now?

Lani

When I went to the doctor's, I knew I was in some deep shit when they said I was already three months pregnant. That was exactly how long ago me and Zamier slept together, me and Ramone's relationship was still rocky so I kept him around. Now I realize me being selfish and trying to be on some payback shit could have cost me my relationship. I couldn't even be mad about him kicking me out of the house. I deserved it but he didn't even try to give me a chance to explain. He acts like he's oh so perfect, he must have forgotten that he didn't tell me about his son that he knew about and decided to keep from me.

I haven't even slept with Zamier since me and Ramone decided that we wanted to work things out. But he doesn't give a fuck, so why should I? My kids and I will do perfectly fine without him. I was good before him so I know I'll be good without him.

I told my daddy about the situation and he was not happy at all. Of course he felt like he had to give me a damn lecture but that's okay, I'm used to it by now.

He helped me to realize my faults and mistakes in the situation. He told me I should have been a woman about the situation and told him how I was feeling. He made me understand that it was very juvenile of me to go on a revenge fuck and mess with somebody else's emotions.

I never looked at it like that. That's why I loved my daddy, he always kept it real and let me know when I'm in the wrong. I had just put Ranyla down to sleep when I got a text message from Ramone.

Ramone: open the door.

I just rolled my eyes while I went to open the door. He was standing there looking sexy as hell with only sweats and a white tee on, but I wasn't going to let him know that.

I just walked to my room without saying a word to him. When we got to my room, I sat on the bed while he closed and locked the door.

"I'm sorry," I said being the first one to speak. "I only slept with him when we weren't together and when I wasn't sure if I wanted to be with you. He was only a revenge fuck and nothing else. I have no feelings for him past a friend level but if this just so happens to be his child, I will allow him to be in its life."

He just looked at me without saying anything. Next thing I know he was taking off his t-shirt and pushed me back on the bed. "I want you and my daughter back home where y'all belong first thing in the morning," he said, pulling my boy shorts off.

Before I could even protest, he dove head first into my honey pot. My hand automatically went to the back of his head. He was sucking so damn good like he was trying to prove a point.

"This shit is mine Le'Lani and if you ever give it away again, I'll kill that nigga," he said right before he made me cum. I was trying to catch my breath when I felt him slide his ten inches in me. All I could do was gasp.

"Tell me you love me," he said placing my leg on his shoulder and going in deeper.

"I uhh…shit. I love you," I said, barely able to talk.

"This my pussy Le'Lani and don't you ever forget that shit," he said, speeding up his pace.

"Turn around," he demanded and I did as I was told.

He slapped my ass before entering me from behind. He grabbed a handful of my hair while he pounding into me unmercifully.

He bent down and placed kisses down my spine and that shit drove me crazy. I was amped up so I started throwing it back, giving as good as I was getting.

"Baby I'm about to cummmmm!" I yelled out.

"Cum then," he said slapping my ass again.

I started to shake and my knees gave out. Not too long after, Ramone followed suit and collapsed on the bed. He pulled me close to him and kissed my neck.

"I want yo ass home tomorrow Le'Lani and I'm not playing," he said.

I didn't respond, instead I just snuggled up close to him and drifted off to sleep.

Micah

Two more months and I will officially be a daddy! I've been waiting for this day for so long. Mykell and Neicey are on their way back up here because Janae just insisted that Neicey comes to her baby shower. I think that it would be good for Neicey to get out and get moving around, especially after all she's been through. When Mykell told me that she tried to off herself I was at a loss for words. Like that shit really cut me deep. She's always so happy, full of life, smiling and talking shit, that nobody would have ever known that she was having suicidal thoughts. I'm happy that she's doing better though because that would have been a hard loss for all of us to handle.

"Baby, come on. We have to hurry up and finish decorating before people start to show up," Janae whined.

"I did not sign up for all this shit," I mumbled under my breath.

"Well you should have thought about all that before you decided not to pull out," she fussed with her hands on her newly spread hips.

I just looked at her and licked my lips. That shit was mad sexy.

She rolled her eyes. "Just hurry up please.

I laughed and shook my head. I'll be happy when this pregnancy is over because these crazy ass mood swings she be having is driving a nigga crazy. One minute she's happy then the next minute she's ready to bite a nigga's head off. *Crazy ass.* I thought to myself.

An hour later, we were finally finished with the decorations. Or should I say I was finished since all she did was sit down and give commands.

"Alright, I'm out. I gotta go pick up Neicey and Mykell from the airport," I said checking the time. Their plane will be here in twenty minutes.

I pulled up to the airport looking for a spot to park. I made it there two minutes after their flight was supposed to get there. I leaned my seat back and waited for them to come out to the car. Five minutes later I heard a tap at the window. I looked up to see Neicey smiling.

"Mack daddy!" Neicey yelled and giving me a tight hug. "I missed you so much," she said.

"I missed you too baby girl." I said hugging her back. "How you feeling?"

She sighed and smiled. "Better, way better. I been going to these meetings that Mykell talked me into going to and they helped so much."

"I'm happy to hear that," I smiled.

"So y'all just gone act like a nigga not standing here huh?" Mykell laughed.

"Nigga please I done spoke to yo cry baby ass every day since you left. Ol attention needing ass nigga," I joked.

"Aw shit, here this nigga go," he laughed.

That's what I loved about my brother. We had an unbreakable bond no matter what.

"Neicey, let me hurry up and get you to the house before Janae blow the whole damn city up with her crazy ass. Y'all women and these damn hormones be driving niggas crazy." I shook my head.

"I wasn't evil when I was pregnant with Romell or Amyricale," Neicey said getting in the truck.

"That's because yo ass is naturally evil," Mykell mumbled.

"Don't think I didn't hear that, nigga," she fussed.

"I love you too."

I just shook my head at the two of them. No doubt about it they were made for each other.

Chapter 21

Mykell

My and Neicey's relationship has been the definition of perfect. So perfect that I'm in a damn jewelry shop getting diamonds added to the engagement ring I gave her a long time ago. This time, I plan on making it all the way. She had been going to some classes to help prevent suicide and help her with her depression. They were a success. The only issues she's having a hard time dealing with is debating on getting an abortion. I told her whatever she chooses to do is fine with me.

I called up Ramone, Lani, Micah, Janae, and both of our dads to help me with a surprise engagement party. She told me that all she wanted was to be happy and me being her man. I have no choice but to make that happen. She doesn't know this but the whole family has been here for a whole week helping set up this engagement party.

Hell, I even made peace with Kamil's ass. There wasn't any sense in acting a fool every time I see that nigga. He made it perfectly clear that he was just cool with being Neicey's friend. He said he would respect our relationship and back up and just be there when she needed him. *That shit won't be happening, that's what I'm here for.*

The plan is to take her to a restaurant and when we walk in, everybody else will be there. We're going to have our own little section roped off. Romell said he wanted to be by a beach so he can write will you marry me in the sand, but MJ said we should use candles to spell it out. I never knew my kids were so damn romantic.

After dropping the kids off at Lakey's, I went to check on the family that I had hidden at the Marriott.

"Okay, y'all ready?" I asked excitedly.

"Nigga, the question is, are you ready?" Ramone laughed.

"Kell, why you so nervous? You act like you ain't never did this before," Lani laughed.

I just looked at her. "Oh you got jokes huh?"

"I'm just playing. I'm happy that you finally decided to get it together," she said.

"You? Shit I've never been so happy in my life. I was getting tired of his ass coming to me crying every day," my pops said.

"Okay, y'all not right. I'm going to my fiancé, at least I know she loves me," I said faking hurt. "I'll see y'all in an hour."

*   *   *

"Mykell why we gotta go all the way to the back?" Neicey asked as we walked towards the back of the restaurant.

"What's wrong you don't trust me?" I asked leading her to the back.

"Yea but..." she stopped when she saw everybody sitting there.

"Hey Ladybug," he dad said getting up to hug her.

"Oh my goodness, what are y'all doing here?" she asked.

"Mommy, come here I gotta show you something." Romell said grabbing his mother's hand. He was so excited that he took her out too early, but that was cool with me. When I saw him take her to the balcony, I crept up behind her and got on one knee.

"What does it say mommy?" Romell asked.

She picked him up, "It's says, 'Will you marry...'" she gasped and turned around.

I smiled and opened up the ring box. Her hand went to her mouth and tears started to fall from her eyes. I looked behind me and everybody was standing there cheering me on, even Kamil.

I cleared my throat. "Neicey, no, Reneice, I know we've been here before but I'm older and more mature now. I'm tired of playing and running around. I want to settle down and have a family, with my family. I don't see anybody else in this world carrying my last name but you. You've stuck by my side when you shouldn't have and loved me unconditionally even when I didn't deserve it. All the shit you've been through would run most women away, but not you, you're still here and I owe you all my love, loyalty and respect. So with that being said, will you marry me?" I asked.

She just stood there crying. Her mouth was moving but nothing was coming out so she nodded her head up and down. "YESSSS!" she finally yelled.

I released the breath I didn't realize I was holding. I picked her up and hugged her so tight. "I promise I'll make it right this time," I whispered in her ear.

She kissed my lips, "I believe you," she said as I put her ring on.

"Umm you guys, I ate to interrupt the happy moment but my water just broke," Janae said before grabbing her stomach.

"Oh shit!" Micah said before rushing to her side. "Are you in pain?" he asked.

"No, not yet," she said.

"Alright, um, I don't know what to do," Micah said running around like a chicken with its head cut off.

"Man, calm down. You acting *yo* water just broke," I laughed.

Janae grabbed her stomach and I'm guessing she just had her first contraction.

"Mack, you gon take yo girl to the hospital or not?" I asked.

"Oh shit, yea c'mon baby," he said, helping her up.

This nigga done been at the birth of every child in this family, now he acting like he don't know what to do.

Janae

It's been four years since I last did this and Lord knows I wasn't ready. I've been in labor for seven hours so far and this little boy acting like he don't want to come out. I've only dilated to 3 centimeters. I didn't have these problems with Ranee, she came an hour after my water broke.

"Micah, I promise you will never touch me again," I said giving him the evil eye.

Everybody in the room looked at me and laughed like I told a joke or something. "What's so funny?" I asked.

"Every woman in this room said the same thing while they were in labor and look at what happened to them. Neicey had another one and Lani got another one on the way," Pop-Pop laughed.

"Pop-Pop, I'm so serious right now. Your son will never touch me ever again, I have toys to take care of that," I said through gritted teeth.

"Don't play with me," he said mugging me.

"I think y'all need to go get some rest. Neicey and Mykell, y'all supposed to be celebrating the re-engagement, not sitting up in some hospital," I said.

"She's right, if anything changes, we'll call you," Micah agreed with me.

"Alright, we're gone," Neicey said.

Everyone kissed me and hugged me goodbye before leaving the room.

"Micah Lamar Jones Jr., you better stop being stubborn and come out so mommy and daddy can see you," I said rubbing my stomach.

*   *   *

Thirteen hours later and still no baby. This is not okay, this has got to be the most stubborn baby ever. Micah was the on the phone talking to Ranee who was asking if her brother was here yet. She's at home in Detroit with my mother patiently awaiting the arrival of her baby brother. All of a sudden out of nowhere I felt a pressure below.

"Micah, call the doctor. I think your son is finally ready to come."

He ran out the room to find a nurse or doctor and two minutes later my legs were being propped up to have a baby. After five minutes, I was finally able to hold my stubborn little man in my arms. He looked every bit like his dad.

"You did good baby," Micah said kissing my forehead.

"No, we did good," I said, smiling at my handsome son.

My family is now complete. I have the man of my dreams with the two most precious kids anybody could have.

Reneice

I can't believe I'm actually engaged again. Hopefully this time I will actually get married. Everything between me and Mykell has been going perfect. I can honestly say that he is my soul mate, I'm truly happy that we worked things out. I was on the floor sitting between Mykell's legs playing with Amyricale when his phone started to ring.

I knew it was Pop-Pop by the way he was talking. All of a sudden, I felt Mykell tense up. I looked back to see a vein sticking out the side of his neck. His hazel eyes got dark and I instantly knew he was upset. *Oh Lord, what now?* I thought as I took Amyricale in the kitchen to get us something to eat. I sat her in her high chair while I looked in the refrigerator.

Amyricale started talking in her baby talk and clapping. I looked over at her and smiled. I'm so happy I made the choice to keep her over a year ago. She really is a miracle; our miracle.

I bent over to get a pot out the cabinet when I felt Mykell behind me. He kissed my neck and I turned around to look at him. He smiled but I could tell he was worried about something.

"Dada!" Amyricale squealed. That's basically the only word that she says.

"Hey baby girl," he tried to walk over to her but I stopped him.

He looked at me and we just stared into each other's eyes for a minute. "Talk to me, what's wrong?" I finally spoke.

He looked like he really didn't want to say. He rubbed his hand over his waves and took a deep breath. "Pops just called to tell me that Candy has been looking for me."

Candy? Not the bitch I had to beat at the hospital? What the hell. I thought.

"Okay...why?" I said.

"She claims that we have a son together," he said in a low voice.

I just looked at him waiting to say he was just playing but he never did. I swear it felt like my heart shattered. *Here we go again.* "How old is he?" I asked.

"Two but I don't think he's mine though, I always strapped up," he said trying to explain himself.

I just shook my head and moved from around him and tried to walk away but he grabbed me. "Neicey..." he was cut off by Amyricale.

"Dada! Dada!" she said with her arms up waiting for him to pick her up. I just snatched my arm away. I grabbed my purse and keys before walking out the door.

Twenty minutes later I found myself at Kamil's. Even with all the bullshit his cousin put me through, I still found it in my heart to forgive him and keep him close to me as a friend.

"Neicey, you need to understand that happened before y'all even thought about getting back together. He's two and Amyricale just turned one. He didn't step out on you this time, you're engaged now so you need to sit down and talk to him about this. You can't always run from your problems," Kamil said after I told him what happened.

I just sighed and thought about what he just said. *He's right.* "I know you're right, let me go home so we can talk about this," I said, getting up and giving Kamil a hug.

*   *   *

When I got home I went to look for Mykell so we could talk. I found him and the kids laying in our bed watching a movie. "Mommy!" Romell yelled. He's such a mama's boy.

"Hey baby," I said kissing his forehead. I looked at Mykell, "Let me holla at you real quick," I said before leaving the room. "MJ, watch your sister and make sure she doesn't fall out the bed," I said over my shoulder.

We walked in the den. Mykell tried to speak but I put my hand up and stopped him. "I'm not mad at you, actually I'm not mad at all. This baby happened before we got back together. We can fly back to Detroit and see him and you can get a blood test done. If he is your son, that's coo,I I'll accept him just like I did MJ."

He looked like he was shocked at what I just said. "We?" he said.

"Yes, we. You're crazy as hell if you think Imma let you go see that bitch alone. You already had that bitch thinking she was wifey, I don't want her thinking that she doing something. I'm the wife, always have been, and always will be," I said.

He just laughed and grabbed me, kissing my lips. "I love you Reneice," he said.

"Don't I know it?" I joked before walking out the room.

"You better know it," he said slapping my ass.

"Pervert," I laughed.

We went back to the room to finish watching *Despicable Me 2* as a family.

Mykell

When I told Neicey about the possibility of me having another baby, I just knew she was going to leave a nigga, *again*. Instead my baby took it like a G and let me know she wasn't going anywhere. I told Candy I would meet her at the Buffalo Wild Wings on Randolph St. Of course Neicey wanted to come, but I had no problem with that. I would know just by looking at the boy if he was mine or not.

"Let me check and make sure I brought my boyfriend," Neicey said going through her purse.

"Yo, I thought I got rid of that damn gun," I said pushing it back in her purse and looking around making sure no one had seen it.

"You did but this is Lakey's," she laughed.

"Crazy ass, always ready to pop some shit off," I shook my head.

"That's because yo hoes always acting up and you be letting em." She rolled her eyes.

"Whatever," I said.

"Yea, whatever," she said, getting up.

"Yo where you going?" I asked.

"Damn, can I not go to the bathroom?"

"Can I come with you?" I asked giving her that look she loved.

She laughed and shook her head. "I already took care of you this morning."

"So?"

She rolled her eyes and walked away, I followed her with my eyes the whole way. Right after she left, Candy walked in looking extra as hell with a damn fire engine red weave in her head. I looked at the little boy that was with her, his head looked like it ain't been combed in forever and his clothes looked like they're two sizes too small. I instantly shook my head. I looked at the boy's eyes and no doubt they were hazel just like the rest of my kids. My heart fell to my stomach.

She walked up smiling like the damn joker. She walked up and tried to hug me I was about to hug her back but I heard somebody clear their throat. I looked to see Neicey standing there. Candy rolled her eyes when she noticed Neicey.

"You could have left yo hoe where she was," Candy said sitting down.

Out the corner of my eye I saw Neicey reaching in her purse. I grabbed it from her and put in on the other side of me. "Watch yo mouth." I glared at Candy.

"I'm the wife, bitch. A hoe is what you are," Neicey said showing off her ring. "Anyways, we don't need a blood test to know that this is his son, but it's pretty clear that you don't know how to take care of a damn child. Look at his head and his clothes. How the hell you step out the house making sure you look good but ya child looking a hot ass mess?" Neicey snapped.

I just sat back and let her say what she had to say simply because I agree with her.

"Bitch, what? I take damn good care of my son! Hell, since you think you know so damn much, have fun raising his ass. I don't have time for a damn kid right now anyways," she said getting up and leaving lil man sitting there.

My damn jaw hit the floor. How the hell can a mother just give up her child like that and not feel no type of remorse. *Trifling ass,* I thought. Niece was cussing under her breath as she walked around the booth to pick up lil man.

"Hey handsome, what's your name?" she asked.

"Tyriq," he said in a low voice, hugging Neicey's neck tightly.

"Hello Tyriq, I'm Neicey and that man right there is your daddy," she said handing him to me.

I put him on my lap and he laid his head on my chest. "Damn, he look just like MJ and Romell," I said looking at him.

"Y'all are triplets. I'm happy Amyricale look like me." Neicey chuckled.

"Whatever man." I laughed with her.

"You hungry lil man?" I asked.

"Yes." He nodded his head.

"Alright, we can eat then we're going shopping, then Imma braid your hair," Neicey said touching his hair. "He got some pretty hair."

"Yes he do. That he gets from me."

* * *

Hours later, we we're back in Florida. Neicey's ass went all out for Tyriq, everything she saw at the mall that she wanted him to have, she grabbed. She treats MJ like he's her son so I have no doubt in my mind that she'll do the same for Tyriq. He takes to her very well.

I was sitting on the couch with Tyriq when Neicey came downstairs holding Amyricale with MJ and Romell right behind her.

"Alright boys, we have a new addition to the family. MJ, Romell, this is your brother Tyriq. Tyriq, these are your brothers and this little one here is your sister."

Romell walked up to Tyriq and handed him his toy. "You want to play wit me?"

Tyriq took the toy and shook his head. "Come on, I show you my room." The two took off running up the stairs and I just smiled.

"Ma and dad, I need for y'all to stop having all these kids. I'm almost fourteen and got like ten brothers and sisters. Oh, I also need for y'all to stop being so loud at night, don't nobody wanna hear all that," MJ said before smirking and running up the stairs after his brothers.

"Imma kill ya son," Neicey said laughing.

"Be my guest," I said as she laid on the couch with me and Amyricale.

I looked at the two most important women in my life and knew I wanted this shit forever. Just the six of us, Tyriq included.

Lani

Today would be the day that my fiancé and my potential baby daddy meet each other. I don't know why I feel so nervous, but I do. Never in a million years would I have thought I would be in this situation; not knowing who the father of my child could be. That's what I get though. I just put on my big girl panties and sucked it up. We have about three months before the baby gets here. Either way the paternity results come out, I know that my baby will be well loved and taken care of. Both Zamier and Ramone are stand up guys and I feel bad about putting them in this situation.

"Hey Meir, thanks for meeting up," I said hugging him. "Zamier this is Ramone, Ramone this is Zamier," I introduced the two.

"Wassup man," Ramone said shaking Zamier's hand.

"First off, let me say that me and Le'Lani talked and we agreed that if you are the father that we would let you be in its life. I have no problem with that. I wouldn't want somebody to keep me from my daughter, so I wouldn't keep somebody else from their child," Ramone said.

"I appreciate that. Lani and I also talked and Imma tell you just like I told her, I respect you guy's relationship. So you don't have to worry about me trynna hook up with her behind yo back or nothing like that. When we did what we did, you two were separated but now that you are back together, I backed off," Zamier confirmed.

"Well since we're not sure who the father is right now, I want the both of you there when I give birth. I would hate for you to miss the birth," I said.

"That's fine but how do you feel about that?" Zamier asked Ramone.

"It's cool," he said.

I sighed feeling relieved. This meeting went way better than I thought it would. Today made me look at Mone in a different light. It reminded me of why I love him so much.

Chapter 22

Two years later

Mykell

In 24 hours I will be a married man. I can't believe it. I'm finally doing it, marrying my soul mate. I was finally man enough to see what I had and know that I refused to lose her ever again.

"Mykell, pleaseeee?" Neicey whined.

"Naw, man. How that sound?"

"It sounds like a good plan to me. Why won't you let me pick the strippers? I already know you gon have some so why not let me pick em?" she pouted.

I sighed. "Alright fine. You win," I gave in.

"Of course I do." She smiled before running out the bedroom.

I just shook my head. *I hope she do a nigga right,* I thought to myself.

*   *   *

I rented out a room at The Biltmore Hotel since that's the same place we'll be getting married. Everybody had their own room. I rented out one for me and one for Neicey since she didn't want to see me before the wedding.

"Man, I can't believe you let Ladybug pick the strippers. She gon have all type of ratchet looking bitches in here," Ramone laughed.

"Shut up man. I trust her," I said trying to convince myself.

There was a knock at the door and everybody got quiet. I went to answer the door but not before looking out the peephole. *Damn,* I thought before opening the door.

"You must be Mykell. Neicey sent us," one of the stripers said looking like a damn goddess.

"Well, come on in," I moved to the side so they could get in.

In walked all types of flavors. Short ones, tall ones, light ones, dark ones, thick ones, thicker than a Snicker ones. My baby did good, I'll be sure to thank her properly.

Two hours into the bachelor party, there was another knock at the door. If I wasn't close to the door, I probably wouldn't have heard it over the music. I opened the door and in walked Neicey, Lani and Janae.

"The hell ya'll doing out this late?" I asked.

"We just came to say hi."

"You mean to be nosey?"

"That too," Lani said.

I followed behind them, watching Neicey's ass the whole way.

"Hey ladies, these fellas treating ya'll right?" Neicey asked the strippers.

"Yes," they all answered simultaneously.

"They better," Neicey said walking over to the bar.

I walked up behind her and grabbed her baby making hips. "You should give a man a lap dance," I said into her neck.

"Boy please, what you think I hired all these strippers for? You better choose one and sit ya happy ass down." She laughed.

"Baby come on, please?" I said kissing her neck. "Besides I heard you a beast when it comes to giving lap dances." I laughed.

She cut her eyes in Kamil's direction then looked at me. "Damn, was y'all comparing notes?"

"Yea and I'm a little jealous but we'll talk about that later," I said slapping her ass.

I moved a chair to the middle of the room and sat in it. "C'mon baby girl, I'm waiting."

"Where the money at?" she asked with her hands on her hips.

"What you mean?" I asked playing dumb.

"Nigga if you in here making it rain on these bitches, you better make sure you make it fucking storm on me." She rolled her eyes.

"Whatever you want baby." I laughed before taking a stack out my pocket.

She whispered something in one of the stripper's ear and suddenly the music stopped.

"Alright ladies, time to pause it real fast while Neicey takes care of her man real quick," a stripper named Asia said. Next thing I know Ciara's Body Part started to play. Neicey smiled at me mischievously before walking towards me seductively.

By the time she was done, I was broke and horny as hell. "Damn," was all I could say. "You coming to my room tonight?" I whispered in her ear while making sure she felt how hard I was.

"I can't. It's bad luck," she said, trying to get away from me.

"Man c'mon Neicey, you can't leave me like this," I said damn near begging.

"It's such a thing as a cold shower." She laughed. "C'mon Kell, stop. I gotta go," she said.

"Go where? It's damn near midnight, where you think you going?" I asked looking at her crazy.

"You had your bachelor party, mine hasn't started yet." She smirked at me.

"What? Aw hell naw!" I said trying to grab her but she was too quick.

"C'mon ladies, let's go!" she called out to Lani and Janae before running to the door.

"Neicey, don't make me fuck you and these Florida niggas up!" I yelled before the door closed.

I just shook my head. *That girl is something else.*

Reneice

I stood in front of the mirror trying not to cry. The day has final come, I will officially be Mrs. Mykell Jones. I just wish my mommy was here to see me.

"Neicey, you better stop all that crying before you mess up your makeup!" Lani fussed at me.

"Lani leave her alone, she has the right to be crying," Janae fussed.

There was a knock at the door. "You ready to go Ladybug?" my dad asked.

"Yea, I'm ready."

"Alright, Lani and Janae y'all are up," he said.

They ran out the room like their asses were on fire.

"You look beautiful, Ladybug," he said kissing my forehead.

"Really?"

"Of course," he said.

"We're up," Pop-Pop said.

I took both of their arms and started towards the doors leading to the hall we were getting married in. I was so blessed to have two very important men walking me down the aisle today.

When I heard "Spend My Life" by Eric Benet and Tamia, I tensed up.

"You okay baby girl?" Pop-Pop asked.

"Yes I'm fine," I said smiling.

The doors opened and I felt my eyes watering. I laid eyes on Mykell and my breath got caught in my throat. He was standing there in an all white suit with a purple vest on. His fresh line up made his newly grown curls look too cute and I got lost in his hazel eyes. Ranyla, Amyricale, and Ranee, the three flower girls looked beautiful. Romell and Tyriq are the two most handsome ring bearers I've ever seen.

I heard "Spend My Life" by Eric Benet and Tamia playing and I started to get butterflies in my stomach. I looked at the two men that I was blessed to have walk me down the aisle as we walked to my future husband. Mykell had a big smile on his face.

When I reached him I couldn't help but let the tears fall, after all we've been through, we are finally getting married. I couldn't be happier.

"Dearly beloved, we are gathered here today to see the union of Mykell Jones and Reneice Peake. Who gives this woman away?" the preacher asked.

"We do," Pop-Pop and my dad answered.

"The bride and groom have decided to recite their own vows," the preacher said.

"Reneice, I knew from the moment I laid eyes on you that I had to make you mine. We've been through so much together from then until now and no matter what, you stayed by my side. You took both of my sons and raised them as yours without any problems and I knew from that moment, you would be my wife. Words can't describe how you make me feel, I'm elated that you would give me the honor of giving you my last name. I vow that until I take my last breath, I will love, honor, cherish, respect and protect you."

By the time he finished I was sure that I had messed up my makeup. The tears would not stop coming.

I sighed before I said my vows. "Mykell, you helped me become a woman. All the good and bad times, I would do them all over again just for you. You gave me the most precious gifts anyone in this world could ever give me. You saved my life and brought me out of the darkness when I never thought I would see the light ever again. I owe you my life. Until the death of me I vow to love, obey, honor, respect, and cherish you."

I swear there wasn't a dry eye in the building. Everyone was crying ears of joy, especially the ones who have been here since the beginning of our journey.

After we were pronounced husband and wife, we shared our first kiss as husband and wife.

"Ladies and gentlemen, I introduce to you Mr. and Mrs. Mykell Jones."

*   *   *

The reception hall was just too beautiful for words. Everything was decorated in white and purple.

"I love you Mrs. Jones," Mykell whispered in my ear.

"I love you more Mr. Jones."

Tyriq and Amyricale came running towards us. "Mommy dance with me," Tyriq said looking like a four year old version of his daddy.

"Daddy dance!" Amyricale said climbing into Mykell's lap.

I just laughed and shook my head. That child is a daddy's girl to the heart.

I danced the whole night away with my family. If I could relive this moment, I would thousands of times.

Chapter 23

Mykell

I woke up to one of the best feelings ever. I looked down to see Neicey handling her business. I don't know what it is but it seems like since we said "I do" she been real freaky. I'm not complaining at all though, I love that about her. I grabbed the back of her head and she slapped my hand away. I laughed knowing she hated that shit. I released a load down her throat and like the true bad bitch that she is, she swallowed it.

"I'll go get breakfast started," she said reaching for her robe.

"Uhn uhn, put that shit down," I said.

"What? Why?" She looked at me crazy.

"I want you to cook just like that, as naked as the day you came into the world."

She just shook her head and laughed. I walked out to the balcony to look at how beautiful the Dominican Republic is. We've been here a whole week and not once have we left this house. I don't care though, the time was well spent with my wife.

I'm a married man! Whoever would have thought that a nigga like me would settle down? I was told that when you got somebody good, you hold on to them. I let my good thing slip away from me once and I'll be dammed if I let that happen again.

I walked into the kitchen and sat at the table while watching Neicey cook. *Damn, she is so beautiful.*

She turned and looked at me. "What?" she asked.

"I'm just thinking about how happy I am that you married me. I mean, look at everything we've been through, everything *you've* been through and you still married a nigga. That's real yo."

She just looked at me and smiled.

"You ready to go home?" I asked as she sat a plate in front of me.

"Yes and no. Yes because I miss my babies, but no because I love it here."

"I feel you, but you know this don't have to be the last time we come here," I said with a mischievous smile.

"What you mean?" she asked.

"I bought this house, this is our shit," I said.

"Oh my God! Really Kell?"

"Yea baby, this can be like our vacation home or something."

"You are like the fucking best." She smiled.

* * *

Six hours later, we were landing at the Miami International Airport. I was laughing and playing around with Neicey, unaware of the two cops that were approaching us until they got close.

"Mykell Jones?" one asked while flashing his badge.

"Yea," I answered.

"I'm Officer Zaluchi and you're under arrest for the murders of Rahkya Martin and Quamal "Boogie" Smith," he said turning me around and placing handcuffs on my wrist. *What the fuck?* I thought to myself.

I looked over at Neicey and she looked like she had just seen a ghost.

"Call my dad, baby," I said as the dragged me away.

Karma has finally caught up with my black ass.

Lakey

I was on my way out with this shorty I had been getting to know when I heard somebody banging on my door. I looked out the peephole and seen Neicey.

"Wassup Snook, what you doing here?" I asked.

"I need you to call Pop-Pop and my dad and tell them I'm about to go to jail."

"Fuck you talking about?"

"The police just picked up Mykell from the airport for killing Kya and Boogie. I'm not letting my husband go down like that LaShaun, I just can't! We've only been married for a fucking week and everything is already going wrong. I'm turning myself in," she said.

"Whoa Snook, look, you need to just sit down and calm down."

"Fuck that! I'm going down there now so you can either call them or not. The choice is yours," she said turning and running to her car.

"Oh shit! Mone gon kill me," I said out loud to myself.

I pulled out my phone and hurried to dial Ramone's number.

"Wassup Lake?" he answered on the third ring.

"Man this is bad, it's all bad. Yo sister done came home from her honeymoon and flipped her fucking wig!" I exclaimed.

"What the fuck you mean?" He asked.

"Al I know is she said the cops picked up Kell for killing Kya and Boogie. She talking about she bout to go turn herself in because she not about to let her husband go down like that."

"Shit!" he yelled. "I'm bout to call my dad and Pops. We'll be there before you can count to fucking ten. Lake go find my fucking sister!" he said before hanging up.

I knew Neicey was serious as hell when she said she was turning herself in. Once she put her mind to something there was no stopping her, so I drove to the police station. When I was about to walk in, Mykell was walking out with a confused look on his face. "What you doing here Lakey?" he asked.

"Man, yo wife," I shook my head.

"What about her?"

"C'mon man," I said walking to the front desk. "Excuse me sir, I was wondering if you have a Reneice Jones here?" I said as nicely as I could.

"Hold on." He typed something on his computer then picked up the phone. He talked in a hushed tone so we couldn't hear what he was saying.

"Lake, man what the fuck is going on and why you asking if Neicey here?" Mykell asked growing impatient.

"Okay, Mrs. Jones just left the interrogation room and is being lead to a cell," the officer said.

"What the fuck!" Mykell yelled.

I just knew some shit was about to hit the ceiling fan.

Reneice

As I sat in this cold ass room waiting for them to come in and question me, I thought about the things people do for love. *They never lied when they said love will make you do some crazy things,* I thought. I'm sitting here willing to take a damn murder charge for my husband. Usually people would feel nervous or something but I don't, I actually feel calm for some reason.

The same officer that questioned me when I was in the hospital walked in. "Alright Ms. Peake—"

"It's Mrs. Jones," I said cutting him off.

"Alright Mrs. Jones, we have somebody who told us that your husband was the shooter but you say it was you. Now tell me what happened."

Somebody told you? The hell?

"Well as you already know, I was kidnapped and was held for about week. The last day, Boogie, I mean Quamal came down the stairs to rape me again when he dropped his gun. I wasn't tied up at the moment so even though I was a little weak, I hurried and reached for the gun. Well, I got to it first and we were fighting over it when it went off. I thought I was hit but when I seen Quamal hit the ground, I knew it wasn't me. The gun shot must have made Kya come downstairs, because she came running in the room. She tried to get the gun away from me and started punching me repeatedly. I aimed the gun and shot her. I shoot her multiple times just to make sure she was actually dead. After that I blacked out and woke up in the hospital," I said with a straight face knowing damn well I was lying through my teeth. Thank God Mykell told me the story about what happened.

"How did your family know where to find you?" he asked.

"Kya told Kamil where we would be and she told him to meet her there at midnight," I said looking him dead in the eyes.

"So you're telling me that you killed them?" he asked with a raised eyebrow.

"Yes, I killed Quamal Smith and Rahkya Martin."

"Alright," his partner said. "We'll take you down to booking then we'll get you in a cell."

I couldn't believe I was actually doing this shit. I've never been to jail a day in my life, well besides to visit my brother of course. The booking process seemed like it took forever. By time I got back to a cell, I was dead tired. Especially since I had that long flight from the Dominican Republic. The cell was funky and cold. I couldn't imagine living like this. If this is what jail is like, I could only imagine what prison is like.

* * *

I had to wake up early as hell the next morning. I was just sitting in my cell daydreaming when they informed me that I had a visitor. I walked in the visiting room happy as hell to see Mykell. He looked like he hadn't had a lick of sleep. I picked up the phone to talk.

"Hey." I said.

"Wassup," he said dryly. "What's wrong with you Neicey? Why would you do some shit like this?" he asked in a low tone.

"What do you mean why?" I looked at him crazy. "Maybe because I didn't want my husband that already has two strikes against him going back to prison for strike three! That's why," I said.

"You're a fucking mother Reneice! Yo damn kids need you. What the hell type of relationship is y'all gone have with you sitting behind fucking bars?" he raised his voice.

I just shook my head at how ungrateful he was sounding right now. "I did this for you and you're mad? Help me out here, maybe I'm missing something."

"You ain't did shit for me. I would have been able to handle this shit. I've been here before so it wouldn't have been nothing for me to do it again. This ain't no place for a woman."

"I can't even fucking believe you right now Mykell. I really can't." I shook my head.

"I'll have Lakey get you a lawyer or something. Don't think for one second that I'm bringing my kids up here to see your ass because it won't be happening," he said getting.

"That's how you feel? You just gon turn you back on me after all I've done for you? Really Mykell?" He just kept walking. I banged on the glass. "Mykell! Don't fucking keep walking away from me. You know what, go to hell!"

To Be Continued

Made in the USA
Lexington, KY
15 April 2016